To
Linda
Best Wishes
Robert S. Kingsley

A Girl Named Sheila

Robert G. Kingsley

VANTAGE PRESS
New York

To a girl of my past, a girl named Sheila

Published by Vantage Press, Inc.
516 West 34th Street, New York, New York 10001

Manufactured in the United States of America
ISBN: 0-533-11665-1

Library of Congress Catalog Card No.: 95-90614

0 9 8 7 6 5 4 3 2 1

1

The clouds hovered low as the wind rustled the leaves from gutter to gutter across Bloomgarden Avenue. The residential street stretched silently and undisturbed by human sound. A lone figure slowly walks the manmade path on this morning. With a raincoat over his shoulder and a grip in his hand, his feet move along the sidewalk like a machine, his eyes glassy and undaunted by any distraction, his mouth tight and expressionless.

As he passes a vacant lot he stops. Putting down his grip he gazes at the lot and a lonely tear trickles down his cheek. For here is where a world started and ended for John Eastman. A joy of a love, a sorrow of death, a little heaven, a little hell. And yet it only seems like yesterday. . . .

* * *

I remember the sun beating down on us as we played baseball on that old sandlot. It seemed funny that such an exclusive part of this small midwestern town couldn't build a little park to keep us kids happy in, but then again I guess nothing could ever replace that old sandlot with the cardboard bases. I thought that I was about the greatest outfielder who ever lived. Well, at 12, who isn't the greatest at something? I remember chasing that fly ball that fateful day all the way to the sidewalk when . . .

"Hey, look out! " shouted a girl pushing a small doll buggy.

"Oops . . . " I uttered as we went head over heels tumbling to the ground, girl, buggy, doll, ball, and me.

1

"Now look what you have done, clumsy."

"I'm sorry. I really didn't see you. Are you hurt?"

"No."

"I'm really sorry you know," I repeated.

"Yeah, you just said that. Well, are you going to pick up my buggy for me or are you just going to leave it there?"

I got up, and brushed myself off and hurriedly turned over her buggy and replaced the doll.

"Hey, Johnny, come on," yelled my anxious teammates.

"Okay," I replied. "By the way, my name is Johnny. What's yours?"

"Sheila," she said shyly. As she said it a grin began to grow into a smile. Her long hair was curled back into a ponytail and her blue eyes sparkled as if they were chips from the stars from the heavens above. I guess I was a little bashful back then because I ran away feeling a little tingly and a little embarrassed as the guys started to tease me. I found myself looking back as she left. She, too, occasionally looked back to see if I was watching her.

It must have been a week later that I was walking home from downtown when I saw Sheila again. She was coming down the block trying not to step on the cracks in the sidewalk.

"Hi."

"Oh, hi," she answered, not acknowledging me as she walked with her head down.

"Do you live around here? I've never seen you around until the other day."

"Uh huh."

"Johnny's got a girlfriend. Johnny's got a girlfriend," teased a few of my buddies as they rode past on their bicycles.

"No sir!" I objected vigorously.

"Johnny's got a girlfriend. Johnny's got a girlfriend," they continued to taunt.

"Cut it out, you guys," I pleaded "She's not my girlfriend. I don't go around with girls."

They rode around in a circle, still chanting. I kept shouting at them but received no reward for my patience.

All of a sudden, Sheila walked over to the boys and, one by one, started knocking them off their bikes. This called for retaliation on the part of the boys, so they started chasing her.

I don't know what got into me but I jumped out in front of them like a log lying in the road and down they came. Turning on me, they commenced to beat the living daylights out of me and left. As I got up with blood running from my nose to my chin and teardrops flowing from my eyes, a handkerchief attempted to repair the damage. It was Sheila.

"This I'm sorry for, Johnny."

She said it with so much feeling that I felt sorry for her. I was bleeding, yet I felt sorry for her? Boy, was I mixed up. First she dried the tears like a tender-loving mother. And in the same gentle manner, and with the touch of a cautious nurse, she wiped away all signs of my blood on her tiny, laced handkerchief. She then stood up.

"I am sorry, honest," she said as she turned and started to walk away.

"Hey wait," I shouted. "Where are you going?"

"Home, I guess," she said without looking up.

"Can I walk you home?"

She turned and looked straight into my eyes. I could start to see the tears form. For the first time in my life I saw loneliness in a person and realized it. I walked up to her side. As I did, she looked down at the ground to hide her feelings from me.

"Johnny, I thought you didn't go around with girls?"

"Well, I . . . "

"Johnny, will you be my friend?" she said asked as she looked up at me. "I mean a real friend."

"Why sure. I guess, anyway. Don't you have other friends?" I questioned.

3

"No. My mother and I are new in Cedar Dale. I usually have to stay around the house and help Mom."

"Where is your dad?"

Her head lowered once again.

"I don't know. I think dead. Well, that's what Mommy says, anyway. He went away one day and we never have heard from him. Mommy keeps hoping, but she says if he were alive he'd come home to be with us."

"How long has he been gone?"

Again she dropped her head.

"A long time. Since I was born, I guess. I never saw him except for the pictures Mommy has of her and him. Do you think he's dead, Johnny?"

I shrugged my shoulders. "I don't know. Gosh, if your mother says so I guess it's so. Right?"

"Right, I guess."

Once again I could sense loneliness. Quickly I changed the subject.

"Now are you going to protect me on the way to your house?" I said, grabbing her hand unconsciously. She squeezed it tightly and slowly looked up. A smile had replaced the gloom and a warmth, of a sort, gripped us as we walked to her house.

2

As time passed, Sheila and I grew up like brother and sister. As I stayed my old self, Sheila changed in many ways. She blossomed into a fine figure of a woman. Her ponytail now hung down to her waist, still as lovely as the first day I saw it. Her eyes still sparkled but now there was no sign of loneliness.

She was now flooded by male companions. If they weren't asking her for dates, they were asking for the pleasure of just taking her home from school. But now Sheila was experiencing a new venture in life called love. Matt Harris was the focus of all her attention.

Matt was a perfect scholar, a fair athlete, and one hell of a nice, modest fellow. I might say also a little absent-minded and bashful.

To illustrate a point, one time he saw Sheila coming down the hall on his way to class and fell down one full flight of stairs when he ran out of hall backing up. Then there was the time he was talking to Sheila and turned around to go to class and entered the girls' restroom by mistake. For that one he almost got expelled from school. But all in all, he was one of the most honest and trustworthy people I knew.

I don't think that Matt was any more excited than a stork after having delivered the wrong baby to the wrong house, than he was when he came to me with some news that everyone else knew weeks ago.

"Hey, Johnny," he said, almost out of breath, "guess who I'm taking to the senior prom?"

"It couldn't be Sheila, by any chance?" I said chuckling.

"Yeah. How'd you know? I just asked her."

"ESP, old man."

"Who are you taking?"

"Nancy."

"Nancy? After what she did to you the night of your birthday party? You got to be joking, of course?"

"No I'm not. Look, she explained to me that instead of getting a ride with one of her girlfriends she walked home, trying to shake a headache she had. She thought the fresh air might help. That's why she wasn't at home where I tried to call her. So everything is all right again. I believe her. Okay?"

"Okay, if you say so, but still . . . "

"Still, schmill. It's okay between us now."

"Hi Matt, Johnny," greeted Sheila as she turned the hall corner.

"Oh, hi," murmured Matt.

"Well, were you going to walk me home, Matt? Or have you something else to do?"

"No, no. I'd be glad to walk you home."

I grinned as Sheila turned her head around to me as they walked away and winked with a smile on her face like a conquering hero or maybe . . . just someone in love. She was happy, and that made me happy, as it always did. I walked away whistling, which echoed through the now empty halls of higher learning.

Finally, the time approached and, like most high-school prom nights, it would be the highlight for the graduating class. I had to get things set up at the school gym since I was on the prom committee and in charge of decorating. This made it impossible for me to pick up Nancy at her house, so Sheila and Matt said they would do the honors for me.

Nancy had been more or less a "puppy love" type of girl for me, but the last few months I felt myself getting more and more serious about her.

"Have you the time to escort a lonely girl to a prom?" said a voice behind me. It was Nancy. She was at her loveliest. Her long black hair draped over her shoulders. The blue chiffon dress she wore accented her bust and her slender hips.

I smiled at her and said, "Just so happens I would be honored to escort a lonely, unescorted girl as lovely as you."

"Gee, I thought the flattery would start much later. But don't stop now."

"Where are Matt and Sheila?"

"Parking the car. They'll be here in a minute."

Just then Matt and Sheila walked through the entranceway. Sheila was so beautiful. I was so proud of her. I knew that Matt was, too. As I remember, once Nancy and I hit the dance floor we just couldn't seem to pull ourselves off it. It wasn't that way with Matt and Sheila. After a while, they left and drove out to the river's edge, to a clearing that all young lovers would go to and park with their best girl.

For two young people in love the setting was right. The night supplied every bit of the mood one would need. Matt shyly put his arm on the back of the seat and with one finger played nervously with Sheila's long, blonde hair. They talked for some time, and both made moves for an unnoticed, better position.

Finally, Sheila looked at him squarely in the eyes and asked, "Matt Harris! Are you going to kiss me or not?"

"Well, I ah . . . I mean . . . " he stammered.

Sheila leaned over and put her arms around him and kissed him. Matt slowly wrapped his arms tenderly around her.

"Oh, Sheila, I've wanted to do that for such a long time. But I didn't want you to get mad at me. And then I thought I might lose you and I didn't want that to happen."

"You won't lose me, Matt. I think a great deal of you. In fact . . . I think I love you."

"Do you, Sheila? I mean really? You know, I've loved you since the first time I saw you last year. I was always afraid to ask you for a date. I thought I'd be no match for all the other guys you had to choose from."

"Matt, if you want something, don't be so shy. I always figured if a person wanted something bad enough it was worth fighting for. Aren't I worth fighting for if you love me? You're worth fighting for to me," she explained, placing another kiss on his lips.

"Oh, Sheila, you are worth fighting for, but what good would it do me now? I can't keep you. It looks like my parents are moving shortly after graduation because my father's job warrants it. It looks like if I win you I'll still lose you."

"Then you'll be leaving soon?" Sheila asked with her head down. "Matt, hold me."

They sat there, embracing, not knowing what to do. In Matt's mind Sheila's haunting words kept echoing, *Am I worth fighting for if you love me?*

Suddenly he took a hold of Sheila and looked in her tear-filled eyes.

"I know this sounds crazy, but if I were to get a room here in town instead of going with my parents and stay on at Mr. Goodyear's grocery store, would you be willing to think about spending the rest of your life with me? I guess I'm trying to ask you to marry me, Sheila."

"Oh, Matt, I don't have to think about it. I will marry you, my darling."

She embraced him tightly and kissed him. They had happiness in their hearts and love had found a home. True love was never so pure. The moon and the trees stood as sentinels and the river moved silently past, unnoticed by the young lovers, for the night was theirs.

They later made their way back to the prom. Standing outside on the steps were Nancy and me. As they came up the steps I asked Sheila to please keep Nancy company while I went around back to get my car.

"Johnny, I think I'm old enough to take care of myself. What's the matter? You act like you don't trust me."

"Oh, I don't mind, Nancy," said Sheila.

I thought I'd take a shortcut and go through the boys' locker room to save myself some time. As I passed through I met one of my fellow classmates.

"Hi, Johnny."

"Hi. How come you're not upstairs dancing? It's almost over, you know."

"I had to get something out of my locker."

"Oh. Well, I got to get to my car out back, so I'll see you later."

When I got to the back door I found it locked, which made me a little upset. So I turned quickly to retrace my route when I heard two voices taking.

"Hey, what did I tell you?" said one. "I told you what was going to happen to that sucker Johnny if Rod had a shot at missy hot pants while he wasn't around. Well, I was right. Rod just picked up Nancy out on the steps out front. I don't know where Johnny was but I'll bet she gives him another one of those famous 'eat it up sucker' excuses, like she did that night of his birthday party when Rod and her went out to their favorite spot down by the old deserted mill. What we should do is go down there and scare the hell out of them. I wonder if . . . "

As I listened I felt a deep hurt, and an anger started to erupt inside me. I guess I was a little out of my head as I jumped out of the protective shadows and on top of the two boys. I pushed all my hurt pride into my fists as I threw blow after blow into one of the guy's stomachs. I saw the other one start to get up. I quickly pushed down on his head and came up swiftly with my knee to his chin. As I saw the one behind me straighten up, I came back strongly with my elbow across his face, knocking him to the floor.

I looked at what I had done but I just wanted revenge at any price. I rushed quickly out of the locker room. As I did I met Matt and Sheila coming down the corridor.

"Johnny, did Nancy . . . Johnny, what have you got all over your pants? It looks like blood," remarked Sheila.

"Not now," I said, running past them and around to the back where I had my car parked. I saw them running out to me as I pushed forcefully down on the gas pedal. My tires ripped through the cinders and the dust rose high in the breeze as I drove out.

My mind was on one thing: the old mill. The mill was long since vacated but was kept as a historical reminder that the town got its name from the many cedar trees that had passed through it. Now it was home only for any parasite or rodent that wanted it. A fitting place to go looking for Rod and Nancy.

I stopped the car a little ways up the road so I wouldn't be noticed. The closer I got, the more doubts I had about what the boys had said, I couldn't see any cars. Was all that a put-on for my benefit? Could I have lost my temper in such a way that I fought for a lie? I silently walked up to the mill. The boards were loose and rotting away. The interior was dark but for a small beam of moonlight weaving its way through the cracks.

There, lying on the dirt floor, as in a moonlit spotlight, were two completely nude bodies. They didn't hesitate to continue, even knowing of my presence in the doorway. Finally Rod turned his head toward me.

"Well, did you come to take lessons from a man? Or did ya just come to observe a stud at work?" he said, smiling as he got his feet.

He was almost face to face with me when a fury inside me unleashed. I brought up my knee hard and swiftly to his groin. As he buckled at the impact I came up with both hands clasped together from about knee-high, and with the force of a mule's kick, underneath his chin, sending him backwards out through the door and into the dirt clearing outside.

Nancy came running up to me, shielding herself as best she could.

"Johnny, he made me come out here. I just wanted a ride around back to meet you at the car but he forced me out here instead. You do believe me, don't you?" she pleaded.

I looked over to where they had been lying and noticed their clothes neatly stacked in a pile.

"It takes two to make a whore. And you're a pro in my book," I said, pushing her outside and into the dirt clearing alongside Rod.

Just at that time a car drove up, shining its lights on Nancy and Rod. They tried to shield themselves as they hobbled back to the mill.

"Johnny! Are you okay?" called Sheila, as she jumped out of Matt's car.

"Yeah. I'm just a little disappointed with the world right now. And I guess at my own judgment."

"Matt, follow us. I'm going to drive Johnny home in his car," yelled Sheila.

"That's not necessary," I said.

"I want to talk to you, Johnny. Come on, let's get out of here."

As we drove a hush fell over the car. Finally, Sheila looked over to me.

"Johnny, don't feel so bad. She's not worth it."

"I know, Sheila, but how could I've been so wrong about a person? I guess a guy in love is blind to the truth and to what everyone else can plainly see. I seemed vulnerable to just about any lie delivered by the recipient of that love. I guess in many ways we live and make our own heaven or hell.

"When I thought I had her love and the plans we talked about were going to become a reality, I found a type of heaven. And tonight, I walked barefooted through the hot coals of a hell I didn't even know existed.

"I thought love was understanding without compensation, forgiving without question. Did you know that love is fought for, sought after, used as an excuse for, and often misused? I think tonight I used them all for my own self-satisfaction. I'm sorry about what I've done this night, but more for the truths of which I have been made aware."

I paused for a moment and laughed at myself. "You know, I'm

11

sure that the sun will not be afraid to show itself tomorrow and time will not slow down in commemoration of this night. Life goes on and so do we. Right?"

"Right! And don't you forget it, big brother," she said, placing her hand on mine.

"Would you like to say something so I don't go on blabbering?"

"Would you like to be cheered up a little tonight?"

"Shoot. I don't mean that for real."

"How would you like to be the first one to know about the engagement of one Matt Harris to your little sister Sheila?

"You're joking?"

"No. Aren't you happy?"

"Yes, of course. But who would have ever thought that Matt could have ever proposed to a girl unless he had a paper to read it off of to make sure he got it right? He didn't read it, did he?" We laughed. "Sheila, I'm so happy for you. I don't think you could have made a better decision. I know he couldn't have. God bless you both. And to think he didn't even ask my permission to marry my sister. How about that!"

I kissed her on the cheek as she gave me a big hug and turned to get into Matt's car. The night seemed a little brighter. My load seemed smaller than it did before. I stood smiling as Matt and Sheila pulled out of my driveway. They drove off down the street sitting tightly together with love in their hearts. The moon hid its face behind a cloud as the night was again theirs.

12

3

With our school days now firmly behind us and the vast uncertainty of the rest of our lives staring us squarely in the eyes, many events started to shape our lives.

In mid-June a very beautiful union between Matt and Sheila took place. She was never so beautiful and Matt was never so nervous. Being the best man, I prompted Matt throughout the whole ceremony. I felt as if I were getting married. Matt was the only one whose pride and joy exceeded mine.

Shortly afterwards, Mr. Goodyear sold his store to an out-of-town chain and went into retirement. But upon his recommendation Matt was placed as the store's new assistant manager. I was glad for Matt because it meant more money and a step up.

As fall approached, I also received some good news. I could not afford to go to college for the pursuit of a career in journalism, so I had sent out many applications to various magazine companies for a type of on-the-job training. To my delight and surprise, one company responded and I jumped at the chance to accept it.

Matt and Sheila had a small house-warming party for the new apartment they had just moved into and I thought I would surprise everybody with my announcement. But I was the one who was pleasantly surprised as Matt announced: "May I have your attention, please," he started. "If you haven't heard, Johnny has accepted a job with a very obscure magazine that, in a short time, will no doubt be number one in the nation due to his fine talents and vast experience. Well, one out of two isn't bad. His absence will be felt by us who love him. We wish him all luck in the world. And I know if we ever need him all we have to do is follow the trail of friends he will surely acquire wherever he may go.

"But, will he ever return to Cedar Dale? Well, Sheila and I think we've found a way to draw him back. What godfather can stay away from his godchild? Johnny, you better start making plans for a return trip around the middle of March."

As congratulations were extended by the guests, Sheila looked up at me. I could see the pride and satisfaction bursting out of her broad smile. I was so very happy for her. She beamed with the radiance that would have put a thousand suns to shame. I didn't have to say anything as she squeezed my hand and gave me a wink, then tenderly gave Matt a kiss. I felt this was surely a gift from God to enrich and reward their love.

The days soon rushed past and I left for my new job. I dropped a few cards from time to time to let her know where I was since my job had me traveling a good share of the time. Soon winter let its presence be known and engulfed everything in sight.

It wasn't until late January that I was close enough to Cedar Dale, and Sheila, that I could call and check on her. She told me how big she was getting and how proud of Matt she was, of how they found a house so they could make a nursery for the expected arrival.

She also said that Matt had been selected to attend a meeting, which was to be held at the owner's home some one hundred miles away. As she told me about Matt having to stay overnight, I could sense a little loneliness and fear in her voice. This would be their first time being separated and she would be so very close to her due date. I tried to ease her gloom by telling her I would see her in March, and how to get in touch with me in case she needed me before then.

As my assignment drew me out of the area I had passing thoughts about Matt on his way to his meeting and wished him luck. But then he had Sheila and her love. How much more luck could one man have?

14

4

As Matt made his farewells to Mr. Hastings, he pulled up his collar on his overcoat. The breeze that swept across the snow was as fresh as the snow itself. He balanced his way along the slippery sidewalk until he reached his car. Once inside he started it up and sat there awaiting the expected warmth from the heater. *It's still early yet,* he thought to himself. *Maybe I'll surprise Sheila and drive on to Cedar Dale tonight instead of waiting until tomorrow. Yeah, that's what I'll do.*

His tires spun as the car moved away from the curb and onto the icy city streets. The heat started to take the cold edge off the inside of the car and the radio became his sole companion as he traveled out of town and on to the highway leading home.

The snow was packed on the road so Matt reduced his speed to allow for it. He figured it was better to be safe than sorry. *An expectant father can't be too careful,* he chuckled to himself. With Sheila so close to the delivery date he figured it was best to be close to her.

Matt sang along with the radio to pass the time. Now and then his car's rear end would slide slightly but he corrected it immediately. His main thoughts remained focused on Sheila and the forthcoming baby. He loved Sheila and now they'd have a little one they both could love equally as much.

Up ahead, Matt could see a car passing a slow-moving truck. He knew it had plenty of time and room so he decided not to slow up. As the car pulled back into the line of traffic the back end started to slide towards the ditch. Quickly the driver turned his wheels sharply, only to throw the car's rearend across the line and into the path of Matt's. Seeing this, Matt swerved out and around, just missing the other car. But in doing so he created an out-of-control condition for himself. He panicked and pushed down hard on the brakes and held them there as everything started whirling around him.

"Oh, my God, my God!" Matt shouted.

A bridge abutment loomed out of the obscure night. The sound of metal scraping and crushing broke into the night's silence. A horn screamed out like a desperate cry for help.

The doorbell awakened Sheila from a sound sleep. Moving very slowly, she put on her robe and went to the door.

"Who is it?" she inquired.

"It's Buff Taylor, Sheila."

Sheila opened the door and the tall slender police chief walked in.

"Buff! What do you want? Matt's not here. He's in Elkton at a store meeting."

"Yes, I know. Sheila, could we sit down for a minute?"

"Sure. Is there anything wrong?" she asked as she stopped and turned quickly around. "Buff, nothing's wrong with Matt, is it?"

"Sheila, sit down."

Sheila shook her head back and forth.

"Buff, tell me. Is Matt okay?"

"He's had a little accident just out of town. I just got word of it and I wanted to be the one who told you."

"But he's in Elkton. He's spending the night there. Are you sure it's Matt?"

"Yes, we're sure. He must have been on his way home. The report I've got is that his car slid into a bridge abutment."

"He isn't . . . " Sheila started.

"No, he isn't dead, but he is hurt bad. I came over to drive you to the hospital."

16

"Oh, Buff. I can't lose him. Not now or ever." Tears flowed like rivers from her eyes.

After she got some clothes on, Buff drove her to the hospital. He helped her up the icy steps and into the lobby. He then led her back to the emergency room.

"Mrs. Harris?" asked an approaching doctor.

"Yes."

"Mrs. Harris, let's sit down here a minute."

"My husband. What about my husband?"

"That's what I want to talk to you about. I believe in being truthful and facing facts. I'm sorry to have to ask you to make such a difficult decision when you are in such a delicate condition. But I have to have your permission for an operation procedure on your husband.

"You see, Mrs. Harris, your husband was in one way lucky and in another way very unfortunate. Lucky, because if his leg hadn't been trapped through the floor boards of the car he would have most likely been thrown to the icy waters of that river and would have been killed.

"But he will have to sacrifice that leg. It's so severely cut and torn that he will never be able to use it again. And it may turn into trouble and a liability later. That's why I need your permission to amputate the leg just above the knee. At least that way, with the help of an artificial leg, he can possibly restore himself back to a productive life."

Sheila wrenched her hands back and forth as tears continued to fall from her cheeks. She looked at Buff.

"It has to be your decision, Sheila," said Buff tenderly as he knelt and held her hands.

"May God and Matt forgive me," she said as she nodded her head yes.

Buff put her head on his shoulder and a dam of tears broke loose inside her heart.

17

Hours passed as Sheila and Buff waited for some news on Matt. Finally the word came.

"Mrs Harris, your husband will be okay. I would like to remind you that we can do the best we can here, provide him with the best care and medication, but I'm afraid that returning to a useful life is going to rest on your shoulders. He needs all the love you can give him and all the moral support you can give him. But stay away from letting him feed on self-pity.

"Right now, at his young age, he could go either way, depending on his mental attitude. At his youthful age he could overcome this handicap or get depressed and wither his life away.

"Like I said, I'll help when I'm needed, but a lot is going to depend on you. You are about to have one of the greatest reasons for living there is."

"When can I see him, Doctor?"

"Have Buff take you home and I'll give you something to make you sleep. You need all the rest you can get in your condition. You can come back later when you wake up. Matt is under sedation right now and won't be awake for some time. By the way, he knows about his leg. I'm not saying that he realized what has happened but he was told when we sedated him to avoid shock and to assure him a good rest. So go home and get a good night's rest. Come back in the morning fresh, lovely, and just the way he'd like to see you, okay?"

"I'll bring her back first thing when she wakes up," assured Buff, helping Sheila to her feet.

They slowly walked toward the hospital exit, only stopping to receive some pills from the nurse. As they entered the brisk fresh air the hint of dawn slowly became evident. Once in the car, Sheila turned to Buff.

"Buff, we've been friends for so long. What shall I do? You know Matt. How will he take it?"

"I really don't know. Something like what Matt has been through no one can truthfully say. Matt's always been shy and sensitive; you know that better than anyone. How this will affect him, I can't say. Like the doctor said, it's going to put your love to the test and push it to the hilt." He smiled at her. "But I think both of you will make it. After all, in just a short time, you'll have proof of your love for each other."

Sheila tried to force a small grin and continued to stare out into the fleeting night as they headed for home. Worried, yet thankful, happy, yet sad. She knew that she had enough love for Matt and with God's help they had a better-than-average chance. They had each other.

5

When Sheila frantically got a hold of my editor he in turn got in touch with me and relayed the news of Matt's accident. I asked for some time off and rushed back to Sheila's side.

For weeks we tried gently and caringly to help Matt accept what life still had to offer him. At times it seemed we had him well on his way to a complete recovery. With work reassuring him that his job would still be there when he returned and the many friends urging him on, and, of course, the day-to-day watch for their eagerly awaited newborn he seemed almost fully recovered. He almost seemed like his old self, at times beaming, when the baby was mentioned.

His regression would start only whenever he heard 'artificial limb.' He told the doctors, in an anger I had never seen in Matt, that he would never wear a stupid, cumbersome falsity like that. Never!

Two days before my return to work and Matt's last week in the hospital before being released to go home, an angel appeared in the form of a five-and-a-half pound baby girl named Robin Rene Harris. It was the greatest God-sent medicine for both Sheila and Matt. I almost needed sunglasses to protect myself from the glow of their happiness and pride.

I kept in touch with Sheila during the weeks that followed and it seemed like everything was working out. She loved being a mother and Matt was adjusting to being a father and having a handicap. It seemed that Robin had been a catalyst, bringing love and happiness back while pushing misfortune into obscurity.

I was able to make it back for Robin's first Christmas but had been unable to attend Sheila's mother's funeral two months previously. Again Robin's presence helped Sheila cope with the loss.

Months began to fall like dominoes off the calendar until Christmas was here again. Sheila and Matt invited me back by dangling a carrot in front of me dealing with some good news they couldn't wait to share with me.

I remember we removed ourselves from the table after Christmas Eve dinner and settled comfortably in the living room.

"Okay, when do I get this great news that you have my interest peaked out on? Or do I have to guess?"

Sheila smiled at Matt as he excused himself. Hurriedly he made his way down the hallway towards the bedroom as fast as his crutches would carry him.

"Did I say something wrong?" I questioned.

"No. Just wait a minute," Sheila answered, with a nervous smile on her face.

I heard the door open down the hall and a figure made its way slowly down the narrow passage. I sensed a faint clicking sound as it moved closer. It was Matt without his crutches. He slowly entered into the light. I saw a smile as big as the sun itself. As my eyes dropped lower I saw two newly shined shoes. He had his artificial leg at last.

"He just got it last week. You're the first to know. Isn't it wonderful, Johnny?" beamed Sheila.

"I've only had it on a couple of times, but I'll get used to it. I need my hands free at work and I need my hands free to hold onto Robin's little hand when we go anywhere together.

"Now I'll be able to do those little things a father needs to do. Like pushing her swing or holding the little doll she loves when she's old enough to climb in the car by herself. You know, stuff like that. And, Johnny, I'm going to learn to drive with it so I won't be such a burden on Sheila."

"You're not a burden," Sheila said jokingly.

"I don't know what to say, Matt. It's the best Christmas surprise I've ever had. I'm happy for you both. Truly I am."

"I've got to get used to it, though. It hurts when I wear it too long, like right now. I'll be right back. I need to take it off."

Matt walked slowly back down the hall and into the bedroom. I looked over at Sheila.

"He's doing better. Are things going good for the both of you?"

"Well, I do feel like the other woman," she said with a grin. "He worships Robin. I don't think he has said no to her since the day she was born. He even gets up in the middle of the night and grabs his crutches and goes in to see if she is still covered. Then he stays in there for about twenty minutes just to watch her.

"He buys her something different all the time, even when our budget won't stretch until the next payday.

"She is also the sole reason he made the decision about getting the leg. He told me that he didn't want her to grow up and be ashamed of him. Lord help us if anything were ever to happen to her."

"Nothing will. She's got the two nicest parents that God ever gave anyone and more love than she knows what to do with," I said as I reached out for her hand.

"I only hope when she grows up she is fortunate to meet a special friend like you, Johnny. If it wasn't for my love for Matt, I think I might have chased after you after we graduated," she said grinning from ear to ear.

"I'll remember that," I joked.

To my misfortune I had to leave Sheila and Matt right after Christmas dinner the next day to get to where my next assignment was. I didn't want to leave, but, with the threat of snow in the forecast, I wanted a head start.

As I drove off, the sun reflecting off the white blanket of snow greeted me. The streets seemed to be void of cars while the children tried out their new sleds, coasting down the few streets that had inclines in Cedar Dale.

But not far away clouds were moving in on the horizon. Little did I know then that other clouds that would change our lives forever were looming over Cedar Dale and Sheila.

6

The spring was really good to me. My first feature article was published by my magazine and they allowed me to go it on my own. I felt good about myself and what I had accomplished in my short two years with the magazine.

I called Sheila once when I was a short distance from Cedar Dale, but I had to stay in pursuit of my story and I hadn't had a chance to stop by.

Sheila told me Matt was only wearing the leg when it was necessary, like for work, to drive the car, or when they went out, which wasn't very often. He was getting another one that fit a little better, she said, and maybe that would allow him to wear it more often.

Summer was again upon us. My thoughts drifted back to Cedar Dale and Sheila.

"Honey, after you get done with what you're doing, would you please bring me out a glass of lemonade?" Matt yelled from the front steps. He was keeping an eye on Robin while she played with her favorite doll and new scooter.

"Sure, just a minute," Sheila replied.

"Thank you," responded Matt as the screen door opened.

"You're welcome," said Sheila as she set down the glass next to him.

"Why don't you sit down and talk to me for a while? I feel I'm getting ignored by both my women."

"After I hang up the last load of clothes I just washed, I'll do just that. Robin sure likes that new scooter, doesn't she?"

"Yes, but not as much as that old rag doll she clings to. She won't go anywhere without it. I guess it was a pretty good investment."

"I've got to get the wash hung out or it won't dry before dark. Why aren't you wearing your leg? The doctor says it's the only way to get used to it."

"I'll wear the new one more when I get it on Monday." He looked at Sheila, who was staring down at him. "I promise."

"Okay. I love you. Now give me a kiss so I can go finish my work."

Matt kissed her and slapped her on the backside as she left the steps. Her eyes returned to Robin as she turned down the driveway toward the street.

"Robin, turn the scooter around. We don't ride scooters in the streets. Want a drink of Daddy's lemonade?"

Robin got off the little scooter and ran up to Matt as fast as her little legs would carry her. As she finished with her drink she climbed down off Matt's lap, causing him to spill the lemonade.

"Robin! Watch it, baby. See you made Daddy spill. Go play while I clean it up, now," he said gently.

Robin walked back out to the scooter but dropped her doll. As she picked it up she bumped into her scooter, causing it to move slowly down the driveway to the street. She saw it gain momentum and ran toward it.

Matt was trying to clean up the spill with his handkerchief, not noticing the events that were taking place. Sheila walked out the side entrance of the house with a basket filled with clothes. As she looked up she saw Robin entering the street chasing the scooter. She also noticed a car entering the street from the near corner. She froze, motionless with sudden fear.

"Robin!" she screamed. "Look out!"

Matt quickly turned his head and saw Robin trying to catch

up with the rolling scooter. He stood up on his one leg and fell in panic. Sheila dropped her basket only to stumble over it as she cried out.

"Robin, I'm coming! Come back, Robin." Sheila screamed, but her pleas went unanswered.

The air was pierced by the squeal of rubber grasping at the concrete street and a horn blaring out a warning.

Matt pulled himself up and hobbled a short distance before falling again to the ground. He then began crawling toward the now-stopped car. Sheila picked herself up and rushed to the now-motionless Robin.

Her little, lifeless body lay sprawled in a blanketing of shattered pieces of the scooter. She lay face down on the cold, gray concrete with scarlet lines of blood moving ever so slowly through the eroded cracks.

Sheila stopped and knelt next to Robin. Slowly she turned Robin over and stared in shocked disbelief. A neighbor assisted Matt over to Sheila's side.

Robin, still clutching her doll, limp and bleeding, forever sleeps. And not even the shrill cry of the shrieking sirens of the ambulance rushing to her aid could awaken her.

Sheila and Matt held each other tightly, both trying to comfort and to be comforted, both cursing and yet praying to God. A mind that can't think and a heart that has no need to, poured out a river of tears, fears, and feelings.

How can this be? Sheila collapsed into Matt's quivering arms as the ambulance aides rushed to Robin's side. Matt thought to himself, *What will life be now without my little Robin?*

A crowd gathered and tears of sympathy slowly trickled through them like a ripple in a calm pond. The small community was touched and saddened. But they could never have dreamed how this would affect the troubled lives of Sheila and Matt.

7

The next couple of months after Robin's funeral found Sheila and Matt growing more distant than ever.

Matt, in self-pity, blamed himself for not watching Robin more carefully, then not saving her. He became isolated and insulated from the rest of the world and, more importantly, from Sheila.

Sheila was in her own world of guilt and emptiness. She tried to communicate with Matt but to no avail. They needed each other, but instead shunned the other's touch and love.

Eventually, Sheila tried to come to terms with her loss by facing the truths. Robin was gone. Now she had to direct all her love toward Matt. Maybe later their lives would heal and maybe, just maybe, they could try for another child. They were still young and still down deep had love for one another.

Meanwhile, Matt tried dealing with life by plunging himself into his work and drinking. He spent many nights late at work or he'd stop by a tavern with Jim, his co-worker. Sometimes he stayed out late so he wouldn't have to face Sheila and discussions about the future. His future was Robin and now she was gone.

"Jim, how about going for a drink after work?"

"Yeah, sounds fine. I want to take you to this one place I found. It just opened a little while back. I know one of the girls over there. Maybe I can get something going. Okay?" questioned Jim.

"Okay. No problem."

As Matt and Jim entered the lounge the live music carried loudly through the establishment.

"There's a table over there," said Matt.

"Just a minute. Come up to the bar with me. I want to introduce someone to you," replied Jim leading Matt to the bar. "Kay, this is Matt."

"Hi, Matt."

"Hi, Kay."

"This here girl is my secret sweetheart. Best barmaid they have in town," smiled Jim. "Where's Julie?"

"This is her night off. But she said she'd be in about now. I get off in about ten minutes and we're going to have a couple of drinks. Then she said she'd drive me home. My car broke down again."

"Why don't you come over to our table when you get off and I'll buy you a couple. Okay?"

"Jim, you've opened your mouth once too often. I'll take you up on your offer, old tightwad." She laughed.

Matt and Jim found a table and watched as the band entertained. A few moments went by and Kay finally came over. She had no more than sat down when another young lady approached the table.

"Hi, Jimmy, Kay." She looked over at Matt.

"Hi," answered Matt.

She was a pretty woman. Her long black hair accented her fine, tanned face. The bow in the back made her look younger than she was. Her blue eyes seemed to smile all by themselves.

"Julie, this is Matt Harris."

"Oh, you're the one I've heard Jimmy talk so much about."

"It's all lies," laughed Matt. "I hope he hasn't said anything too bad."

"No, on the contrary, very nice things. And I bet you're a good dancer, too."

"I used to be fair but I had a little accident and haven't done much lately," explained Matt.

"Nonsense. Once a good dancer, always a good dancer. Do you like fast music or slow?"

"Slow, but . . . "

"They're playing a slow one now. Prove me wrong."

The challenge was very tempting, so together, they proceeded to the dance floor. When they reached the floor Matt looked at Julie and smiled as he said, "Now remember, I warned you."

They began to dance, at first very slowly and definitely. Then, like the moves of an athlete limbering up, the steps became more natural. The more they danced, the closer he held her. As they moved closer to the bandstand, Julie looked up at the bandleader and smiled. "Hi, Gene."

"Hi, Gene! Sounds like a clean name," commented Matt.

Julie laughed and pressed closer to Matt. As the music stopped they went back to their table.

"Well, was he as bad as he thought?" inquired Kay.

"No. He's a very good and graceful dancer. He's easier to follow than some of the 'fancy dans' that hang out around here. Do you live in Cedar Dale?" Julie asked Matt.

"Yes. Jim and I work together. Or rather, I work and he puts in his time."

"Hey!" chuckled Jim.

As the music started again, Matt asked Julie to dance once more. After they had left the table Kay turned to Jim.

"Is he the one you were telling me about who lost his little girl?"

"Yeah. She ran out in front of a car. Matt still blames himself because he refused to use that artificial leg he's wearing now. He couldn't run fast enough on the crutches he had to get to her in time. The police told him that even with two good legs he wouldn't have made it in time. But you can't convince him of that.

"He still gets depressed a lot. I notice it quite a bit down at the store. That's one reason I thought I'd bring him over here. By the looks of it, Julie might be the right medicine for him," he said as he glanced out to the dance floor.

As time passed, they each parted company. Julie began to leave and turned around to Matt.

29

"Are you coming back sometime, Matt?"

"Would you like me to?"

"Yes," smiled Julie. "Yes, I would, very much." She then turned and walked out.

"Nice girl, right?" asked Jim.

"Very nice," answered Matt. His eyes followed her out. "What was her last name?"

"Klingman. Julia Klingman."

"I must remember that," smiled Matt.

All the way home, Matt stared into the star-brightened sky and whistled the haunting music that they had danced to earlier.

When Matt reached home he started to feel a little guilty. But, he thought to himself, why should he feel guilty if there was nothing to it?

As he lay there in bed next to Sheila, Julie's face kept appearing in his mind's eye. He would probably never see her again anyway, so why even think of her? She was just a pretty face who tried to make a cripple feel a little better. That's all. Or was it?

A few days later, as Jim was leaving the store, he poked his head into Matt's office.

"Hey Matt, want to go over to the Sandpiper and grab a beer?"

"Afraid not. I promised Mr. Hastings I'd get this quarterly report done. Then I think I'll head home."

"Okay, old buddy. But, if you change your mind, I'll be there. I think Kay and I have something going. You haven't been out since we were over there two weeks ago. All this work will kill you. Remember, all work and no play makes Matt a very dull boy. But your married guys are like that," laughed Jim as he waved good-bye.

Later, as Matt headed for his car, he ran though his mind, *I wonder if Julie would be there at the Sandpiper? Oh, leave well leave enough alone.*

All the time he headed for home, Julie's face haunted his inquisitive mind. A block away from home he slowly stopped. He thought for a moment, then turned the car around.

She probably won't be there, but I'll have one beer with Jim then go home, he thought, trying to justify his decision.

He entered the lounge and saw Jim at the bar talking to Kay. He strolled up to the vacant stool next to Kay and asked, "Is this one taken?"

"Yes it is," came a soft voice from behind him. He turned around, and there stood Julie.

"You know, you leave your seat for just a moment and some stranger wants it," she said, smiling.

"Hi. How you been?"

"Compared to what?" joked Julie.

"Jim over there."

"Probably a lot better. He's lovesick. I haven't seen you around for a while."

"The store keeps me busy, among other things."

"Do you still dance, or did you forget how?" she said as she slid her hand into his. Then she led him onto the dance floor.

"It's strange, but I've been thinking about you ever since we met. You are a very attractive woman."

"Is your wife attractive?"

Matt stopped in surprise and looked back at Julie.

"Yes. Yes, she is. You know I'm married?" he questioned with some reluctance.

"Yes, Kay told me. She also told me about your little girl. I'm sorry you lost her."

With moisture gathering in his eyes and a faraway look in his gaze he held her closer as they continued to dance.

"Forgive me for mentioning that. I only wanted to let you know I knew and I'm here if you ever need someone to talk to," she said, looking into Matt's eyes and gently squeezing his hand.

He pulled her closer and the music seemed to bond them together as no more words were spoken.

Each day started the same between Sheila and Matt. A little

idle conversation with Sheila trying to mentally inch closer. And, every time, Matt would reject her because he would look at her and think of Robin.

At night he was working later, not at the store but at the Sandpiper. Almost every night he didn't have to work late at the store you could find him at the Sandpiper with Julie.

As they had done many times that night, Matt and Julie again walked to the dance floor. Julie placed her head firmly on Matt's shoulder and they danced silently across the floor. She lifted her head and looked into Matt's eyes.

"You know, you could be so darn easy to fall in love with."

"Don't. Everything that I've held dear to me has turned to shit. I don't ever want that to happen to the happiness we have." Matt's voice was soft but unyielding.

"What if it's too late?" questioned Julie, with a small smile and eyes sparkling.

Matt didn't say anything. He just held her tightly and kissed her forehead.

"Matt, do you think you could find it in your heart to love me? I don't ever mean as much as you do Sheila, but a little? I do love you, even if you never love me. I think you know that."

Matt stared into her eyes and felt the words she had spoken had truly come from her heart. He also knew his feelings toward her. But the words couldn't come.

He was partly afraid he might hurt her and that was the last thing he wanted to do. And partly the awareness of his situation as a married man stopped him. He loved Sheila. But how could he do the things he'd done? How in the hell did he ever fall in love with Julie? It wasn't planned, that's for sure.

He thought of all the heartaches and broken dreams that he and Sheila had shared. Sheila was always there to remind him of the pain while Julie represented the only happy moments he had had since Robin's death.

Maybe he was wrong in what he was doing. Maybe not. He

held Julie a little tighter and they danced as if they were the only ones on the floor.

Suddenly, Matt looked into her eyes.

"God help you, Julie, for I do love you, too."

Julie kissed him with mixed emotions. Hearing the words that she had longed to hear had only brought her joy. Yet, a bewilderment possessed her. She did not understand Matt's plea for her. They had found love, a forbidden love, in each other's arms and hearts. But where to now?

"Matt, please don't ever do anything to hurt me. I love you too much and that could be very bad for me," said Julie, her eyes closed as she held Matt very close to her.

"Honey, I'd never hurt you intentionally. I promise."

They danced on through the night satisfied with the knowledge of each other's love.

At home, Sheila hung up the phone and reached for a piece of paper and a pencil. She quickly scribbled out a note to Matt so he would know where she had gone. Placing it on the table, she slipped into her coat and left the house.

It was a very nice night out, thought Sheila, wishing Matt didn't have to work so late so he could share it. She was glad she had told Sandy she would walk over to her house instead of Sandy driving over to pick her up. As she walked she breathed deeply the invigorating winter air.

The blocks dwindled away as she passed the Sandpiper Lounge. As fate would have it, she glanced in the large, plate-glass window. There sat Matt next to a very attractive girl she had never seen before.

She started in but hesitated. Many questions flashed through her mind. Why wasn't Matt at work? What was he doing in there with a strange girl? Or did he even know the girl?

She slowly walked to the opposite side of the street and leaned up against a tree. Suddenly she started to feel guilty. What if he didn't know the girl? What if he caught her spying and it all turned out to be harmless? Was she letting her mind run away with her?

She then started away from the protection of the tree. She stopped. Her face was expressionless as she noticed Matt and the young lady leave their seats and walk to the dance floor. The girl, smiling, turned toward Matt and put both arms around his neck as they danced slowly and tightly across the floor.

Sheila's heart seemed to collapse as tears began to form in her eyes. Her whole world had shattered. Her stomach was in knots and every nerve in her body started to shake in protest.

She turned away and commenced walking toward home and its sanctuary. The snow crackled under her slow, mechanical steps, which turned into a pace, then a trot, and finally into a sprint.

She swiftly opened the door and ran into the bedroom. Tossing herself across the bed, she sobbed with rejection and bewilderment.

"Matt, oh, Matt, why? I love you so much! Why? God, help me to understand what I have witnessed this night. I don't want to lose him, too. Oh, Lord, please help me, please."

She muffled her cries as her tears dampened the bedspread and stained her heart, her pride, her trust, and, most of all . . . her love.

8

The sun's gentle rays softly touched Sheila's tear-swollen eyes as the alarm clock beckoned a new day. She turned over to Matt, who had only recently arrived to his position alongside her in bed. She got up and walked to the bathroom to wash her face and try to ease the tell-tale signs of the night before.

Matt rubbed his eyes and slowly arose, drained of energy.

"Good morning," she calmly said, trying to conceal her pain. "I'll go put the coffee on."

"Yeah, okay," slurred Matt, who was sitting on the edge of the bed. "I sure need some."

"Rough night last night?" she inquired.

"That bookkeeping's a killer, but it has to be done."

Making his way from the shower to the kitchen, Matt was guided by the scent of breakfast to an awaiting Sheila.

"Matt, we haven't been out for a long time and Sandy and her husband want to have a drink with us after work tonight. Or do you have other plans?" she asked coyly.

"Uh . . . well . . . not exactly. I guess we could go out and have one," he answered, as a glimmer of guilt touched his conscience. "Sure, I'll try to get done early and we'll go out."

When Matt left for work, Sheila called Sandy to invite them for an evening out. Then, nervously, she watched the long minutes and hours pass. She tried not to think about last night, but as she saw the images in her mind the pain grew and again the tears fell unmercifully.

Sheila was dressed and waiting as Matt pulled into the drive-way. She made her way cautiously to the car, forcing a smile.

"Where do they want to meet?" he questioned as he pulled into the street.

"They want to go to that new place over by their house. I forget the name. It's something like Pied Piper or something like that."

"You mean the Sandpiper?" Matt asked, gripping the steering wheel tightly as his body tensed.

"Yes, that's it. I hear they have live music," she said shyly.

"But we'll never be able to talk in there with all that noise going on. I'll run in and tell them we'll meet them somewhere else."

"No. I want to hear the music, too."

Matt's mind was racing as fast as it could to find another reason for not going to the Sandpiper. But before he could, they were in front of the lounge. He stopped and turned off the motor. He sat in hesitation and confusion. What if Julie was in there? How could he explain it if she came up to him?

"Are you coming?" asked Sheila, sliding out of her side of the car.

Matt sluggishly exited the car as Sheila grabbed for his hand so she wouldn't slip in the frozen snow.

"Your hand is shaking. What's wrong?" asked Sheila.

"Nothing, just . . . just a little cold—that's all."

As they entered the lounge Sheila's eyes searched for Sandy. Matt's eyes were frantically scanning for Julie. By the time Sheila had found Sandy, Matt had surveyed the lounge and saw that Julie was not there. A sigh of relief and a smile finally eclipsed his pale face.

After some drinks were ordered Sheila turned to Matt. "Do you remember how to dance?"

"I can't dance anymore with my leg."

"Oh, yes you can. The doctor said you could do just about everything you did before the accident. Including dancing."

Matt shook his head. "I'd probably step all over your feet. No, I don't think so."

"Let me be the judge of that," she said as she arose and took Matt's hand.

She led him to the dance floor as he once again scanned the room. While they danced Sheila stared into Matt's busy eyes.

"Matt, you know I love you, don't you?"

"Of course I do. What a silly question."

"No. I mean, I really love you. The kind of a love we had the night of the prom. The kind of love we had for Robin. The kind of a woman has for a man when he's done something wrong but forgives him when he is honest with her."

"What makes you say that?"

"I just wanted you to know. And you still dance beautifully. Have you been practicing?" she said interrogatively.

He held her close and all his guilt seemed to manifest itself in his mind. Uncomfortably he finished the dance and helped Sheila back to her chair.

He stared at her. Did she suspect or did she know? His thoughts turned to Sheila's feelings. How could he have been so heartless and uncaring as to have created such a situation? Not only could it ruin his marriage but most of all deepen the hurt she already bore with the loss of Robin.

As they sat silently at the table, Matt reached for her hand and tenderly placed it between both of his. With a small frog in his throat and his lips quivering, he spoke to her.

"Sheila, remember above all I have loved you all my life. I may not have been the perfect husband or . . . father—" his eyes reflected the moisture of a gathering pain—"but I have dealt with my hurt while ignoring yours for a long time. I must tell you. . . . "

At that moment a familiar voice interrupted.

"Matt, how's it going?" It was Jim. "First time I've seen you and your beautiful wife out and about. You got a hard worker there, Mrs. Harris."

As he spoke, Kay walked up alongside him accompanied by Julie.

"This is my girlfriend, Kay and her friend, Julie," he continued.

"Hello," Kay and Julie said in harmony.

Sheila right away recognized Julie as the girl who had been with Matt the night before.

"Hello," Sheila responded watching Matt's and Julie's eyes trying not to make contact.

"Well, we have to go now. We're trying to make the last movie before it starts. See you at work, Matt."

"Yeah," Matt replied, a little lost for words.

As they walked away, Matt's eyes couldn't help but gaze at Julie as she looked back while exiting.

"Do you know her?" questioned Sheila.

"No. I mean, I think I've seen her coming into the market. But I'm not sure."

"She acted as if she knew you. Now what were you saying before we were interrupted?"

"Oh, I think that was all. Do you want to go home? I have to get up early tomorrow."

"I guess so," Sheila uttered disappointedly.

While driving home neither one spoke at all. When they reached the front door Matt unlocked it and reached for the light switch. Sheila's hand intercepted his.

"No! Leave the lights off."

"Why?"

"Matt, kiss me. Not like you had to but like you want to. Hold me tightly and kiss me."

With only the streetlight reflecting on the white layer of snow penetrating the darkness, two silhouettes merged into one shadow. Their lips met, first ever so softly, then deeper and more intense.

"Make love to me here and now." She spoke with some urgency in her voice.

They both knelt as Matt gently laid her down while slowly

removing her clothes, then his, as he softly kissed her. She rolled him over to assist him with his belt and lowered his pants down to his legs.

She kissed him as she gently mounted a very excited lover. A few moments passed and, well into their love-making, Sheila asked, "Do you ever get this excited when you dance with Julie?"

"What?" a startled Matt replied.

"Did you get this excited last night while you were dancing with Julie? Matt, I saw you last night."

Matt lay motionless and speechless.

"You're not going to deny it, are you?"

"Deny what? So I stopped in for a few beers and danced with someone. Big deal. What were you doing spying on me anyway?" Matt argued very defensively.

"Matt, you're impossible," she said as she gathered her clothes and headed for the bedroom. She turned with tears in her eyes and pleaded, "Please sleep out there tonight. I don't want you in here right now."

The door slammed shut, but the words stayed in the air like stagnant cigarette smoke.

Matt stayed on the floor and stared at the ceiling, reflecting on the events of the evening. He had come so close to telling Sheila about Julie. Why had they picked that moment to stop by? Sheila had been telling him all night, with bits and pieces, giving him a chance to make a clean breast of things.

Why was he so dense? he wondered, as rolled over and beat his fists into the rug. The night passed slowly and sleeplessly for Matt.

For Sheila it was a night like the night before. Tears and pain gripped her in her moment of anger. The trust they had was gone. The honesty they had was gone. The love they had for each other, was that also gone?

As always, the darkness would hide her from her fears and comfort her, if comfort could be found this night.

9

Sheila opened her eyes as far as they would go. The sunlight rushed to greet them through the partly opened drapes. Her chest felt hollow and empty from all the crying.

She slowly vacated the bed, which had been her sanctuary last night and cautiously opened the door. Peering into the living room she found it empty. Where had Matt gone?

Now a new feeling introduced itself. The thought of the void of being alone.

The front door opened slightly and Matt appeared, holding a handful of roses. He noticed Sheila.

"Let's talk," he said with a wavering voice. "Please."

They both sat down on the couch. Matt grasped her hand as if she were going to fly away.

"I want to finish the talk I started at the Sandpiper last night. You were right. I do know Julie. I did dance with her the other night. I don't know why I denied it last night.

"The truth of the matter is I've been spending a few nights down there. A few! No, many nights. When I said I was working late I went there.

"Please don't ask me how or why it got started; I just don't know. I guess I could blame it on many things and many people but I alone am to blame.

"Sheila, I love you as no one in this world can. I know I have seriously damaged our marriage. Our life together may be beyond repair but the only way I can show you I'm truly sorry is by being truthful with you at all costs. I never wanted to hurt you, believe me.

"I want to come back to you, if you'll have me. I know that any promises I could make now won't be accepted because I've lost your trust.

"However, I do promise you that what was ever between Julie and me is gone and buried. I'll do anything to get you back."

"Matt, I have to know one thing. Did you sleep with her?" questioned Sheila, hoping for the truth but not knowing if she was ready for the answer.

Matt, with tears forming in his eyes, tried to find an easy way to be honest but not brutally harsh with Sheila's feelings. He could only utter one word: "Once."

Anger and betrayal compounded her pain. With her head lowered, tears began to fall on her hands like a gentle rain.

Matt sat with his head bowed in shame while gripping her hands ever so tightly. The only sound in the room was that of their sobbing. Only thoughts of love, lies, and solutions occupied their minds.

The minutes seemed like hours, with no one moving a single muscle, until finally Sheila raised her head and slowly squeezed Matt's hand. He lifted his head and they stared at each other momentarily.

"Matt, I love you. You're all that I have, but I have too much pain in my heart for you to be in there right now.

"I love you, I don't want to lose you, but this is going to take a little time and a lot of work to get back to where we were.

"You're right about one thing, the trust we built our love on has suffered major damage. And, yes, any promises you make will leave a doubt about their being real.

"But if our love has been real and been strong, we can weather it. Until then, business will NOT be as usual. Slowly and together is the only way we get past this."

She stared into his eyes as silence captured the moment.

"Hold me, Matt. Nothing else, just hold me."

She closed her eyes as Matt gently put his arms around her, like someone caressing a bouquet of delicate flowers. In her solitude Sheila prayed for the pain to pass, her love to last, and forgiveness for them both.

She had Matt back for now but for how long? Forever? Or until Julie appeared again?

10

For the next few weeks Matt walked a tight, self-imposed line, neither working late nor stopping for a drink. He even went out of way to keep from going past the Sandpiper by driving down the next street over.

He and Sheila would turn on the radio and play cards or play some other game together, trying to gather some one-on-one feelings. Some nights they would just sit on the couch in the front room and talk. Talk was the one thing that had been missing since Robin died.

Gradually, a held hand here and a tender moment there, a kiss, a hug and a sense of reliability began to slowly mend the heartache.

A small town is a hard place in which to live down memories and mistakes. Matt found this out as he was walking downtown trying to search for a birthday gift for Sheila. As he turned to enter the door at the local clothing store he ran into Julie coming out.

"Hi, Matt," greeted Julie.

"Julie! Hello," Matt replied, somewhat startled.

They stared at each other for a moment.

"Jim told me why you stopped coming into the Sandpiper. Hope everything is going okay for you now," she asked, as if to pry a little.

"Fine. Yeah, just fine." Matt's mind was a complete blank.

"Like I told you once before, if you ever need someone to talk to, I'm still there."

Matt started to feel guilty that he was even talking to Julie. After all, he told Sheila he would have no contact with her.

"Got to run. Call me sometime. See you later. Bye," he said rushing off with his heart nervously pounding.

"Bye," Julie replied disappointedly.

Matt entered the store and quickly lost himself in the crowd. As he looked back he saw Julie walking away. He hesitated for a moment, then continued looking for a present for Sheila.

Later on that night, as they went to bed, Matt saw Julie's face every time he closed his eyes. Why did he have to run into her? Everything was starting to go so well. And why did he make that stupid remark, "call me some time"? He didn't mean it. Or was it his heart calling out from his subconscious? She was still as beautiful as ever.

He tried to put her out of his mind and the battle waged until sleep released him. At least for tonight.

Another couple of weeks passed and there was only an occasional thought of Julie until. . . .

"Hey, Matt, there's a call for you on line one," yelled one of the stockboys from the front of the store.

Matt picked up the receiver. "Hello, this is Matt Harris. May I help you?"

"I hope so," came an all-too-familiar voice. "This is Julie. I hope you're not mad at me for calling you at work, but I want to say good-bye. I'm leaving Cedar Dale and I wanted to let you know I understand about you going back to your wife. But . . . I wanted you to know I'm still in love with you, for all it's worth. I guess I just wanted to tell you one more time before I left."

"Leave? But where are you going?" Matt questioned, with a hint of panic in his voice.

"It's best for both of us if you don't know. Matt, I wish all the best for you and I'll miss you. I love you more then you'll ever know. "Bye, Matt."

"Julie! Julie!" yelled Matt, but only the sound of the dial tone greeted him. He slowly hung up the phone.

With a faraway gaze in his eyes, he leaned back in his chair. Dazed by the sudden news, he sat motionless. Was he the reason she was leaving? Why did she have to call? Was it to punish him?

The more he thought, the more he remembered the happy times with Julie: The time they first danced together. The time they confessed their love for each other. His thoughts became more and more confused by the moment.

This was good news for Sheila and Matt, but he was losing Julie, perhaps forever.

Bewildered, he paced back and forth in his office. Should he chase after Julie and stop her from leaving? Or be thankful she was gone?

Now that Julie was leaving, he decided he needed Sheila more than ever. He announced his departure from the store and rushed home.

As he entered the door Sheila was just coming in to the room. He took her into his arms and held her close to him.

"Well! What is all this about?" Sheila asked smiling.

"I just wanted to hold you. I love you, Sheila."

"I love you too, Matt," she said, holding him tightly.

In his arms he had the love he cherished and needed. But in his mind he only thought of the love he had lost.

Weeks passed by and the Midwest summer's heat slowly increased Matt's need to stop in for a cool drink at the Sandpiper. Sitting at the bar were Kay and Jim.

"Hi, you two," greeted Matt.

"Why, hi, stranger. How goes it?"

"Fine. And you?"

"Great. Jim and I were just talking about you. Were your ears burning?"

"No. Just my throat." Matt laughed.

They sat there for a while making small talk and then Matt asked, "Where was it Julie said she was going? I can't remember."

"Arlington Heights, on the north side of Chicago. I thought she wasn't going to tell you."

"She didn't. I just needed to know, Kay. I still think about her. She's a hard girl to forget."

"Look, Matt, I know this none of my business, and I don't want to cause any more grief than you have had to deal with, but I know Julie called you before she left. How much did she really tell you?" quizzed Kay.

"She called me up to say she was leaving and that she still loved me. That's all. Why?"

"Well, it's not really my place to say this, but do you have any idea why she left?"

"I could only guess. She probably couldn't stand to be in the same town with me after the way I shunned her."

"No." Kay paused and laid her hand on Matt's. "Julie couldn't stay here because she loved you enough to not make it harder on you and Sheila when she has the baby."

"Julie's pregnant?" stammered a wide-eyed, shocked Matt.

"Yes," spoke Kay, in a soft, tender voice. "She figured a small town like Cedar Dale would make it rough on you and Sheila if she stayed. You know . . . she did love you that much." Kay gently patted him on the hand.

Speechless, Matt turned and walked slowly toward the door. Outside, he opened the car door and fixed his eyes toward the heavens and muttered, "What have I done? Julie, please forgive me."

11

With the passing weeks, summer moved on as fall's cooler temperatures and beautiful artistic colors changed everything in sight.

Matt also began to change, into a chameleon. When he was with Sheila, he was a loving and caring husband. When he was alone, he became a dreamer with thoughts of Julie.

One night, as Matt turned out the lights and locked the doors to the grocery store, he zipped up his coat to protect himself from the crisp night air. He pulled himself into his car and turned on the radio as he started it up. He pulled out into the flow of traffic as across the airways came the song Julie and he used to dance to.

Just thinking about her caused him to become depressed. He decided to stop and have one drink before going home to Sheila.

As he entered the lounge his eyes searched for a seat. He found one at the bar. The jukebox was turned up so the people who were dancing could hear it above the chatter of the other patrons.

"What'll it be?" asked the bartender.

"Brandy on the rocks, please."

As he waited for his drink he noticed the girl at the end of the bar. She reminded him so much of Julie he almost thought it was her. Her hair, her eyes, and her mouth were Julie's to a tee.

"Say, who is the young lady at the end of the bar?"

"I really don't know. She came in last night alone and left alone. Tonight, looks like the same thing. She came in alone and is still sitting alone."

"Give her a drink and ask her if she'd care to join another loner."

The bartender delivered the message. Much to Matt's surprise she picked up her purse and joined him. They talked for a while, but Matt stared at her hardly hearing a word that was spoken.

Even when they danced he felt as if he were holding Julie and no one else. He missed her so much, but what could he do?

The hours passed and the young lady left the bar, again alone. Matt sat there, drinking and playing records on the jukebox.

If only he could see Julie again. In his heart he felt a pain. Why didn't hadn't she told him why she was leaving?

The hour was very late when he walked from the bar to his car. He slowly pulled out onto the street, the street that would take him home but not away from his thoughts of Julie.

Again the radio gave him sounds of remembering. Songs that only Julie and he had shared and that made him miss her just that much more.

His mind whirled with perplexing questions and inadequate answers. Nothing fit together.

Suddenly he stopped the car. He knew of one question that could have just one answer. If he loved her so much, then what was he doing here? He must go and find her.

He turned his car around and headed for the airport. He must find out. If she loved him like he loved her why should they ever be apart?

Meanwhile, at home, Sheila tossed and turned, occasionally looking at the clock. Her anxieties grew into worry. Her bewilderment turned into concern. Picking up the phone, she dialed the police.

"Hello, is Buff Taylor there?"

"No. He is out on patrol right now. Can I help you?"

"Yes. When he calls in will you have him get in touch with Sheila Harris as soon as possible?"

She put down the phone and put on her robe. It seemed like hours before there was a knock at the door. It was Buff.

"What's the matter, Sheila? I got your message. Is there anything wrong?"

"Buff, Matt's not home yet. He told me he'd be home right after work and that was five hours ago. He's been pretty true to his word lately. I'm worried something may have happened to him again."

"Don't you worry. I'll go check around and see if I can locate him. Why don't you go back to bed so when he does come home, he won't be worrying about you losing sleep over it."

"Okay," smiled Sheila.

As Buff's car pulled away from the house, Sheila sat down in the living room window seat. She sat there staring out into the night.

She sat there gazing as the black of night slowly turned into dawn. There came a knock at the door. Buff was back.

"Did you find him?" she asked as she noticed another car pull into the driveway. It was Matt's car but Matt wasn't driving it.

"Sheila, honey, let's sit down a minute."

"Matt's not hurt again, is he?"

"That's just it. I don't know," answered Buff. "We found his car at the airport parking lot with this note to you on the seat."

Buff placed in her quivering hands a small, folded piece of paper with her name on it. She slowly opened it and began to read it aloud:

My Beloved Sheila,

Please don't worry about me. I have a great problem on my mind and I must get away for a while and figure it out. I know this will add to the large amount of misery I've caused you already, but it's for the best, for both of us. I'll explain later when I see you. Please forgive me, my love, and try not to hate me too much. Take care of yourself for me. Until I see you again.

With All My Love, Matt

As she looked up at Buff, tears rolled from her eyes. Her voice was unsteady and uncertain. What had she done? What was she going to do without Matt?

She let Buff out, thanking him with what reasoning she had left in her mind. Quickly she ran to her bedroom and threw herself on the bed and wept like child. Where could he have gone?

"Matt, Matt, my darling, please come back. I love you so much. I can't think of living without you.

"Oh, God! Give me strength to understand. I feel like I have lost a part of my heart, my being, my reason for existing. Oh, please, dear Lord, take special care of my Matt because I love him so. And please bring him back home to me. I love him so much."

But her tears and pleas were not heard by Matt this night. He only heard the straining motors of the plane that was taking him to Julie.

12

As soon as Matt landed at the airport, he hurriedly gathered his coat and departed the airliner.

In the lobby he saw a telephone booth. Fumbling for change with one hand he lighted a cigarette with the other. He dialed the operator.

"Operator."

"Yes, do you have a listing for a Julia Klingman? I don't know the address."

"Just a moment please. We've a listing for Julia C. Klingman at 530 Dawson."

"That's it," replied Matt quickly. He now felt anxious and very excited, realizing he had almost found her.

Jotting down the number and address he put in another coin and dialed. The phone rang and rang but to no avail. Matt's smile vanished as he hung up the phone. He slowly walked out of the airport lobby.

Standing out in the cold night wind he looked again at the slip of paper he had written her number down on. The address. He had her address on the paper, too. Having renewed hope, he flagged a taxi.

"Five thirty Dawson street, please."

The taxi driver drove him to an attractive new apartment building. Matt asked the cabby to wait while he ran up to check the apartment.

Searching through the mailboxes he found Julie's number. He knocked on the door, but no answer came from the darkened interior. He knocked again. This time the door of the next apartment opened.

"Are you looking for Miss Klingman?"

"Yes, I am. Do you know where she might be?" inquired Matt.

"Why, yes, She and her roommate mentioned they were going down to The Bramble Bush to dance. They wanted me to go but I had to watch the neighbor's kids."

"The Bramble Bush?"

"Yes," replied the young lady.

"Thank you."

Matt ran back to the taxi with the information. A few moments later they pulled up in front of a small night club.

He walked with his eyes searching everywhere for Julie. No Julie. He scanned the booths. No Julie. He looked over to the bar. No Julie. Had he missed her? If so, where could she have gone?

He turned slowly to walk out. As he did he glanced over his shoulder once more to look over every face on the dance floor.

He suddenly stopped in his tracks. There she was. How ever did he miss that face before? Placing his coat on an empty table, Matt made his way through the dancing couples until he reached her.

"May I cut in, please?" he said, tapping her partner on the shoulder.

Julie looked up. Her mouth appeared expressionless as her eyes reflected all the joy that was rushing up from her heart at that moment.

"Matt, how . . . " started Julie.

"Hush. I'll explain later. Now just hold me and tell me you're glad to see me."

"I am, oh, I am," she gasped, as tears began to form in her eyes. "I love you much, please darling, don't leave me ever!"

"Hear that song they're playing? 'For all we know we may never meet again.' Honey, I'm not taking any chances like that ever again. I found you and I never intend to let you go again. Never!"

He held her close and kissed her forehead gently.

"I'm not holding you too tight, am I?" he said.

"Why did you ask that?" questioned Julie, looking into Matt's eyes.

"I don't want to hurt the baby."

"How did . . . "

"I know and I'm very happy. Now I have two to love. And you never looked so radiant, Julie. When?"

"There will be three to see Christmas this year. Until then, hold me in your arms. Never let me go."

"Never."

They embraced and slowly glided across the dance floor as one person. Julie looked at Matt and, trying to smile through her tears said, "You, Mr. Harris, are stuck with me. And thank God I have you, my love."

Matt caressed her as they kissed. Julie placed her head on Matt's shoulder and the world was again a wonderful place because of two happy hearts. They felt the warmth and the joy of love.

And yet, many miles away, a heart that at one time knew the same warmth and joy now only feels emptiness and loneliness.

13

Weeks turned into eternities for Sheila. Her heart was heavy and pounded excitedly at every ring of the phone, with the hopes that this one was from Matt.

I didn't know what had happened until I called Sheila that November day.

"Hi, little sister. How goes the battle?" I said cheerfully.

"Oh, Johnny," she said, sounding as if she were about to cry. "Matt's gone."

"What do you mean, gone?"

"Gone! Buff found his car at the airport with a note saying he loved me but he had to resolve a problem he had on his mind.

"I don't know where he went or if he's still okay or anything. Johnny, I'm so lost without him."

"Did Buff say anything was missing from the car?"

"Just the little rag doll of Robin's. He always carried it in the car seat next to him.

"I hope he's not thinking about Robin's accident again. Who knows what he might do if he gets back into that state of depression again."

"Do you want me to come back and look for him?"

"No. Not right now, at least. I'm going to give him a little more time. I know when he's ready he'll come back home to me. I have to believe that. Don't I, Johnny?"

"Yes. But, please call me when you hear from him. I'll check back with you from time to time. Okay?"

"Okay. Johnny, what would I do without you? I love you, big brother."

"I love you, too. I'll call you later. Bye."

"Bye," she said, as her pain traveled through the phone lines. I felt so bad and so helpless.

I felt I had to find out more of what had transpired. Maybe there was something Buff wasn't telling Sheila to shield her from any farther pain. I picked the phone back up and called Buff.

"May I speak to Sheriff Taylor, please."

"This is Sheriff Taylor."

"Buff, this is John Eastman."

"Oh, hi, Johnny. What can I do for you?"

"Buff, I just got done talking to Sheila . . . "

"Yeah. Bad situation, isn't it? You know, I thought things were coming together for those two after all their problems with losing their kid and that stepping out that Matt did on her and—"

"Wait a minute. What do you mean, Matt stepping out on Sheila?"

"Well, as I heard it, Matt found a little cutie down at one of the local lounges and had a little affair. Sheila found out about it and put the kibosh on that. Ever since, things looked like they were looking up for those two," Buff explained.

"Who was the girl?" I asked.

"Don't know for sure. I think her name was June or Julie or something like that. But she left town shortly after that."

"Did Matt know where she went?"

"No. Don't think so. Once he and Sheila tried to getting things back together, he pretty much stayed away from her as I heard it."

"Where do you think he's gone?"

"To tell you the truth, I don't know. I figured at first it was just a weekend to iron out a solvable marriage problem. But it's been weeks. I've put out an APB and notified all the hospitals for over a hundred miles in all directions but we've had no luck.

"You know, he's even lost his good job over this disappearing act. No, I just don't know what was on his mind at the time."

While everybody was wondering about Matt, many miles away Matt only thought of Julie and the baby that was on the way.

Occasionally he thought about Sheila. He knew he could never go back. But still there was a pain in his heart when he thought of her.

Twice he tried to call her but hung up when she answered. Both guilt and fear consumed him upon hearing her voice. He also found a sort of solitude from just hearing it, too.

Matt caringly joked with Julie about how well she carried the baby, not really showing until this last month. They laughed and shared moments that only expecting can bring. And they were happy.

They packed the suitcase she would take to the hospital when it was time, together. They spent hours planning her wardrobe for both going to and coming from the hospital, together. They moved things around the apartment to make way for the new baby, together. These were good feelings and ones captured by their love for one another.

"Julie, I've decided to ask Sheila for a divorce. Then we can get married," announced Matt.

"Are you sure? I mean, I want you, but I'm just as happy as I can be as long as you're with me."

"No. I want the baby to have parents and my name."

"The baby will have your name whether we're married or not. I love you, but I don't want you to marry me just to give the baby your name. I love you and so will the baby. Just love us and never think of leaving us."

"I'll never leave you. There is nothing on God's green Earth that will ever take you from me. Only God Himself can ever separate us," Matt said holding Julie tightly in his arms.

He knew that this was the woman who would share his life and with whom he would grow old together. Together forever.

As they sat on the small couch in their apartment, they watched the warm sunrays diminish as the sun sank out of sight, letting the November chill mass into the darkening night. But they feel no chill, just the warmth of each other's arms.

The next few days wore greatly on Matt's mind. He was fighting with the decision on how to ask Sheila for the divorce. He sat down with pen and paper to write to her but couldn't find the words that would let her release him from this now faded love. With every reason he could give why he should leave her, his thoughts released many more why he should stay. Nothing ever reached the paper.

Maybe, he thought, he should phone her and explain. But then he'd never be able to find the words once he heard Sheila's voice. What should he do?

Then, it happened.

"Matt, please call a taxi."

"A taxi? Why?"

"I think it's time." Julie smiled, trying to hold back her discomfort.

"Oh . . . oh! Are you sure?" exclaimed Matt, as a momentary state of shock gripped him.

"Yes I'm sure. My water just broke, so hurry."

Matt called for a taxi and quickly gathered the prepared suitcases for the hospital. A smile of happiness encompassed his face he gave Julie a gentle kiss.

"I love you. Forever, I will love you," he said.

"And I, I mean we, will love you forever and beyond, my darling."

As they reached the hospital, an attendant rushed Julie away. Matt filled out some papers for the hospital then retired to the waiting room.

It seemed like an eternity as Matt paced and finally came to rest by a window. Staring into the darkness he remembered when Robin was born. And Sheila, how beautiful she looked when she was pregnant. And how happy they were on the day Robin was born.

His thoughts deepened about Sheila.

"God help me and forgive me, for I still love Sheila. Lord, please watch over her." A tear slowly moved down his cheek.

"Mr. Harris?" came a soft, intruding voice.

"Yes."

"Mr. Harris, I'm Dr. Barnett. Could we go in this empty room for some privacy?"

"Is there something wrong?"

"I'm sorry to have to tell you this, but the baby was stillborn. We think she probably . . . ."

"She?"

"Yes, it was a girl. We think she probably had respiratory problems."

"Does Julie know?"

The doctor paused for a second, then opened the adjoining door. In walked the hospital chaplain.

"I'm very sorry, Mr. Harris. We lost your wife a few moments after the delivery. I'm assuming she told you of the possible chance she was taking by carrying out the full-term pregnancy and delivery? I told her when she started seeing me to talk to you about it. She convinced me you were well aware of the risks involved."

"She never mentioned any risks to me," mumbled Matt, drowning in a sea of shock.

"It's just a miracle she was ever able to conceive in the first place," the doctor continued. "I'm terribly sorry if you didn't know, and I feel torn by your loss. I will leave you with Chaplain Miller and you can stay in this room as long as you need. If you need me please don't hesitate to call. Again, I'm deeply sorry."

As the doctor walked out of the room and closed the door behind him, the chaplain sat down across from Matt, who was in a state of shock and total disbelief. The chaplain handed Matt an envelope addressed to him by Julie.

"She asked me, a couple of weeks ago, to hold this for her and give it to you if something went wrong." The chaplain spoke in a soft, comforting voice.

Matt quickly took the envelope and stared momentarily at it before gently opening it.

My Dearest, Darling Matt,

If you are reading this it means that I can't be with you now. But my love will always be with you.

Please, focus on what I'm about to say and please don't hate me, my love. I'm not going to tell you of my medical history but I was told a long time ago I could never have children or even conceive.

Matt, when I met you, you'll never how many bells and sky-rockets went off in my head and my heart. I've loved you from the moment I was introduced to you.

I've never known anyone in my life that I felt more complete with than you. When you held me either while we were dancing or just in an embrace, the rest of the world held no meaning or purpose. I figured I was safe from any hurt or pain I might encounter when I experienced my biggest hurt, which was finding out I was barren.

Then that one, wonderful night we shared together in Cedar Dale produced a miracle. I even had two different doctors check me to make sure.

I came down to the Sandpiper to tell you the night you brought Sheila in. When we left I think I cried for two whole days without stopping.

Then I thought to myself, I still have proof of our love inside me. The doctors tried to talk me into terminating it but this was the only thing I had left of you, my darling. I just couldn't, at any cost.

I left Cedar Dale because I wanted your happiness above all even if it was with Sheila and not me. After all I still had a part of you.

I will never be able to find any known word to describe my

jubilation and surprise when you showed up on that dance floor that heavenly night. I felt that God was working overtime to make my life perfect.

There are not very many times in this life that you can get everything you hoped and prayed for. But I did.

I pray our love was strong enough so you can understand why I had to try to have our baby. And I hope it's strong enough for you not to hate me but to feel happy for me, happy for us, for I will still be with you always. Just close your eyes and I'll be there.

My dearest, please take the same love you gave to me and share it with our child. It is you and it is me.

Forgive me and love me. Until we meet again, all my love to you both.

Julie.

Tears began to fill Matt's eyes. Folding the letter slowly, he bowed his head.

"Shall we pray to our Lord God almighty, to ease our pain?" said the chaplain placing his hand on Matt's shoulder.

"What God? He doesn't hear me. He doesn't know me. He doesn't love me. What has He ever one for me but bring me pain and suffering?

"He has taken Robin from me. He has taken my leg from me. He took Sheila from me and now He's taken Julie and the baby from me. What more does He want of me?" screamed Matt.

"I gave Him my love and He gives me His spite. What have I ever done to Him that He has to take everyone I love?

"He can't give me comfort because He knows I blame Him for everything that has happened. I loved him. Now He shits on my life. He's taken the heart and soul from me, why . . . why, then, should I ask anything of Him?"

"Because He is God. Because Julie believed in God and His mercy and His wisdom. She believed in Him so much He gave her you and a chance at happiness and she was fruitful again.

"She also believed in you, Matt. Or, maybe she might have

been wrong about how strong the love was that you two had. If she wasn't, then thank God for love. Thank Him for the merging of your two souls and thank God that He chose you to give Julie that perfect life of which she spoke.

"Curse Him in your pain if you must but He will still love you and forgive you. He has just allowed Julie to go and prepare a place for you when you next meet.

"Don't shut Him out for He will be with you always."

Matt buried his face in his hands and cried. His world had collapsed around him. Now he had no one. He now felt that it surely was true that everything he touched or loved was then forever tainted by his misfortune. A feeling of shame and blame engulfed him.

As he left the hospital he wandered aimlessly through the streets, leaving a single trail in the bed of freshly fallen snow. The snowflakes touched his cheeks, but he could not feel their chill. He could only feel the hollowed-out emptiness and compressed confusion that gripped him.

These were the same feelings held by Sheila many miles and prayers away.

14

Matt never did go back to the apartment. He wandered around the town in a daze. Not knowing anyone, he spent most of his time the next couple of weeks in and out of bars.

In each bar a song, a face with soft, flowing black hair, would only remind him of Julie and the pain would rage from within.

He slept where he could, only getting his meals out of a bottle. Wandering constantly and condemning his very existence, he submerged himself in self-pity, sinking past the life of a nomad.

With Christmas swiftly approaching, the streets welcomed busy shoppers and crowed walkways. More snow began to fall to chill even more the bones of the lost and depressed.

Weary and tired, Matt struggled to lift one foot at a time, only to place it back down in the freezing snow that covered the sidewalk. His mind was hazy and thinking became a bitter battle.

The wind whipped down his coat collar, pushing floating snowflakes ahead of it. His hands had found some sanctuary in the shallow warmth of his pockets. As he passed the still-lit store windows, he paused to take a look himself.

Is this Matt Harris? It looks like a bum, he thought to himself. His hand left the warm pocket to touch his beard-covered face. He readjusted his coat to eliminate a little wind.

Suddenly, he noticed his figure was not the only one present in the reflection from the window. Now there was a little girl and her mother standing alongside of him. The girl's face slowly changed into Robin's for a moment, then changed back. Matt's eyes started to accumulate tears and they soon rolled down his cold, unshaven face.

The little girl looking into the window slowly turned her head backward to look up at Matt.

"Mommy, why is the big man crying? Huh? Why?" she asked in all her innocence as she pulled on the hem of her mother's coat.

"Hush. I don't know. It isn't nice to talk about people, so you just never mind," answered her mother.

Matt quickly turned his head and tried to dry his tears and replace them with a smile. He turned back around but there was no one there. The smile vanished as he began to walk away.

His heart hung heavy and was breaking into little pieces. He turned into a nearby alley. Halfway down, his eyes emptied a flow of tears that represented all the hurt inside of his aching, bleeding heart. A heart that once held hope and happiness now only hid agony and despair.

"My God, my God," he cried, pounding his head and fists against the brick, frost-covered wall. He beat the wall with great, forceful blows with his fists until blood trickled down his knuckles and fingers.

Falling to his knees in the snow and slush, he cried like a little child lost in a troubled world. For his troubled world was without any one of his loves.

Finally pulling himself together, Matt walked slowly out of the alley. Looking at his hands, with the blood partially dried and frozen, he reached down and picked up some snow to wash it off and soothe the pain. He reached for his soiled handkerchief to wrap around one of his hands.

His eyes focused on a small café across the street. His bad leg had stiffened up but, hobbling across the street, he approached the entrance. The knob of the door even seemed to greet him with an icy reception. As he jerked his hand back from the knob the door opened and two patrons made their exit.

Matt looked around the dimly lit place. The table and chairs had seen better days and the booths were cigarette-stained with initials carved everywhere. But the warmth was worth it all.

Matt picked out a booth, dragging himself over to it. As he reached into his pocket and pulled out his money, a new fear gripped him. Only fifty-five cents to starvation.

"What'cha having, Mac?" inquired a gum-chewing similarity to a waitress.

"Huh? Oh . . . coffee, please."

"One cup of joe, Hank," yelled the woman, with lungs that would put a drill sargeant to shame. When she brought the coffee she asked if there would be anything else?

"Yes, please. May I have a pencil? . . . Please."

The waitress gave him a pencil and walked away. Matt took care in pulling a napkin out of the holder. Unfolding it, he began to write:

My Dearest Sheila,

Please forgive me my love. You probably hate me but in my heart you will always stay. I've sinned greatly and put on our love, marriage, and lives a dirt that is almost impossible to erase.

I feel that I'm living in my own-made hell and will never see the part of heaven I had when I had you.

Sheila, please forgive me. I'm trying to find it in my heart to, in some way, ask God to forgive me for my blaming Him for all my misfortunes.

I've lost everything in this world that I've ever loved. First Robin, then you, now Julie and the baby and, most of all God. I blame myself for not being a man, not only physically but mentally, too.

I can't come home, even if you'd have me, until I've made my peace with God and my own mind.

Oh, God, how I miss you, though. You're in my every thought, every dream, and every prayer. I get so lonely at times that I could kill. . . .

Matt's hand stopped and his eyes stared steadily at the booth across from him. He put down the pencil and started to fumble with the fifty-five cents lying on the table, and he continued to stare.

Looking down again at his napkin-letter he started to fold it with the care one would take with a priceless scroll. Sliding it into his pocket he arose and slowly walked to the door. His eyes hardly moved as he made his exit through the same door that had let him enter.

Once back out on the street, he searched for anything that might give him help with what he knew he had to do. He walked for blocks in the cold; then he saw it: Pawnshop. He walked in and looked around for some time. He approached the dealer.

"Can I help you?" said the dealer.

"Ah . . . yes. Can you show me something in a small revolver?"

"Yes, right over here. This one is in very good condition and I know it works because I personally know the fellow who brought it in. His wife made him get rid of it because she was afraid of weapons of any sort.

"Only ten dollars," he said as he was giving Matt the once-over. "We must have some identification also with every purchase of a firearm. Policy, you know. Do you have some?"

"Yes, yes I have," answered Matt, as he fumbled around for his wallet.

Just then, by a stroke of luck or fate, the phone rang. The dealer looked away for only a second while reaching behind him for the phone; Matt picked up the gun and started for the door.

"Hey, just a minute there!" shouted the dealer, grabbing at his coat.

Without thinking Matt turned and brought the gun sharply down across the dealer's forehead. A sudden pang of panic surged through him as he ran from the pawnshop and down the nearest alley.

Leaving by the opposite end, he slowed down to a walk and intermingled with the Christmas shoppers on the busy street.

But what good is an empty gun? he thought to himself. He started to walk past a hardware store but stopped and wandered in. It seemed that all the sales help were busy with other customers.

Matt made his way over to the gun department and found the shells locked in a glass case. Just then a salesman came over to the counter.

"Yes, sir, can I be of some service?"

"Yes. Do you have .32 caliber shells?"

"Yes sir, right over here," he answered, opening the glass case. He took out a box and handed them to Matt.

"Oops . . . " murmured Matt as he dropped the box to the floor spilling out some cartridges. "Sorry, I guess my hands are still a little cold."

Matt reached down and started to put the fallen shells back into the box, but not before he palmed one cartridge.

"How much for a box?"

"The price, I believe, is right on the box."

"Oh! My, but I didn't realize they were that high. I'll have to think about it," Matt said, as he handed the shells back to the clerk. He turned back and walked out into the shifting, cold night wind.

Turning again into an alley he inserted the shell into the chamber. He thought to himself, *This is what I have to do, but can I, can I?*

Water once again started to form in his eyes as doubts formed in his uncertain mind. He reached into his inside pocket and withdrew the little rag doll which his little Robin had talked to so many times before her death.

"What shall I do? Oh, God, what shall I do?" shouted Matt. "My Sheila, my tender, loving Sheila. If I could only talk to you one last time. I don't know what to do. If I could just hear your voice.

"If I thought maybe you could forgive me and would take me back . . . maybe . . . if only I could talk to you for a moment I could find strength enough to go on.

"Yes! If only I could talk to her, maybe . . . she would forgive me and let me come home. I'll call her. Yes, that's what I'll do, I'll call her. Right now."

A glimmer of new hope surfaced as Matt wiped his eyes. He put the gun in one pocket and the doll in the other.

Stumbling out of the alley's shadows, he scanned the street for a phone booth. Spotting one on the lonely end of one block he made his way toward it. He entered the booth, still wiping his eyes, his face trying to fit on a slight smile.

He started to search through his pockets for his money. Where was it? He had it. Frantically, he clawed at every pocket.

His face stiffened, as if it were made of stone. Now he remembered. He left it all on the table at the café.

Depressed and bewildered, now he knew. He felt that God had not forgiven him and didn't want him to reach Sheila or anyone.

He slowly pulled out the doll and kissed it as a tear fell on it.

"Good-bye, Robin. Please forgive your daddy."

Suddenly a muffled sound was heard and Matt slumped over, grasping the doll. Then he released his grip . . . forever.

Sheriff Taylor got in touch with me through my editor and told me what had happened. I told him to let Sheila know I was on the way to Cedar Dale. I had to take a bus since my car had given out on me a few weeks prior.

Buff, related the whole story to me as it came in over the wire service to his office. He said he only told Sheila that they found Matt dead. And since he was still holding onto Robin's doll that he must have been depressed over her death.

The rest was withheld and filed. I appreciated Buff's candor in shielding Sheila from any more unneeded pain.

My only thoughts were of Sheila and her grief. I prayed for each mile to pass quickly so I could be by her side and add what comfort I could. I couldn't help but wonder what Sheila was doing that very moment as I looked out into the night from my speeding bus.

Sheila sat in the window seat where she and Matt had sat so

many times before. She gazed out of the window to the freshly fallen snow. The moon's luminescence made every flake resemble a small jewel sparkling and glistening with high brilliance. A single tear slowly rolled down her cheek. She raised her head toward the heavens.

"Dear God, have I sinned so much that You hate me this much? I thought I could bear no greater sorrow than that of losing little Robin. It's one of the heaviest burdens I've ever had to bear. But now You've taken my Matt away from me, too.

"Why, oh, Lord. Why? It's hard to live or think about living without love. I did love Matt very much and I always will, you know that. I just can't fathom why all of this should happen to us just when we were all so happy. Why? Why? . . . " she sobbed as she buried her head in her hands.

Even with the lights off, as she raised her head, Sheila's eyes reflected the pain of it all.

She glanced over to the picture of Matt holding Robin. A smile of a sort crossed Sheila's face momentarily as she remembered how happy they were once. Walking across the room to the picture, she picked it up. Holding it close to her, she poured out the tears that come only from a lonely, broken heart.

Walking back to the seat in the window she sat down again. Looking at the picture again in the moonlight she whispered, "Oh, how he loved her. And oh, how I loved them both."

Sheila, once again, hugged the picture and cried herself to sleep. And the night passed.

15

The day was hot and sticky, summer had surely arrived. There was hardly a hint of a breeze in the air as Sheila strolled along the small beach area that she and Matt had gone to so many times in the past.

The water was calm and drifting along so very slowly. She sat down on the sand and put her feet into the cooling water and gazed over it.

Her thoughts were of happier times on this beach. Happy times with the school kids on their parties. Happy times alone with Matt. Then happy times when they brought Robin down with them. How long ago it seemed to be.

"Matt, why did you have to go away? I need you so badly."

"My name's not Matt and I don't plan on leaving right yet. So, if I'm not intruding, would I do?" came a voice from behind her.

She turned her head around and looked up. There stood a man, with a fine build, in a bathing suit, with a towel around his neck. He also wore a pleasant smile that had a great deal of warmth and sincerity, one like Matt used to have.

"I didn't mean to startle you," he continued, "but I thought for a minute you might be talking to me since the beach is vacant except for you and me."

"I was just talking to myself," Sheila explained. "I've done a lot of it lately."

"Well, I guess a little friendly conversation to yourself doesn't hurt anything, as long as you don't start answering yourself. Then the people with the little nets and the white coats will come and take you away.

"Then I think I'd feel so bad because I'd be the only one on the beach I'd probably start talking to myself. And if I should answer just one little question they would come with those same little nets and white coats and—"

"I get the idea," giggled Sheila. "I promise never to answer myself so you won't be taken away."

"Now, that's downright friendly of you. By the way, my name is Earl."

"Just Earl?"

"Just plain Earl."

"Okay. Mine's just plain Sheila."

"Sheila! My, but that's a beautiful name. It fits you. It really does, honest."

"How did you find this beach? I thought it was sort of a forgotten place."

"Well, truthfully, I got lost and stumbled on to it by mistake."

"You're new around here, aren't you?"

"Yes. I'm here to organize a selling corporation for a product I'm associated with. I imagine I'll be here for some time. It looks like a nice little town."

"Cedar Dale? Yes, it's a nice little town, all right."

"I don't suppose I could intrude upon you to be my companion for dinner tonight, could I? I mean, being in a strange town I feel a little hopelessly lost and lonesome.

"And if I feel too lonesome, I'll start talking to myself and then start asking myself questions. Then I'll answer myself and—"

"I know, I know. They'll come and take you away."

"Well, how about it?" he asked, sitting alongside her.

"I really can't, but thank you for asking. I don't go out very much any more. Besides, I have a few things to get done around the house. And I hardly know you."

"A husband waiting for you at home, right?" he questioned.

"No." She paused for a moment. "My husband died a few months ago," she replied, her eyes slowly gathering moisture.

"Oh, I am very sorry. But I would be most honored to have a very attractive lady, like yourself, sitting across from me tonight.

"Your home duties couldn't possibly wait until tomorrow, could they? I don't mean to be a pest, but look at it this way. If I knew you longer I wouldn't be a stranger, right?"

"Right," smiled Sheila.

"And if I wasn't a stranger I'd most certainly would be your friend. Would you turn down a friend?"

"Well, I . . . I guess maybe not but . . . "

"The only thing that stands between strangers and friends is time. Time to get to know each other. So if you'll take time to have dinner with me tonight we could become friends instead of becoming strangers."

"There must be logic in there somewhere but I can't seem to find it," said a puzzled Sheila.

Sheila thought to herself that she hadn't been out of the house socially since Matt's death. Maybe a dinner out would be okay. He seemed nice enough.

"It would be dinner and nothing more?"

"Just dinner and conversation. That's all," smiled Earl.

Sheila thought a moment. "Just plain Earl, I accept your invitation for dinner."

"Fine. I'll pick you up at six, okay?"

Sheila nodded her head and gave him her address. They talked together for a while and then he left.

She began to get nervous on her way home, not knowing if she had done the right thing. She had turned down a number of friends who asked for dates and now out of a clear, blue sky she had accepted a date with a complete stranger.

But this is what she was told to do by many of her friends. Besides, the damage had been done now anyway.

Earl picked her up promptly at six o'clock and took her to the best supper club in town. They ate and danced and laughed a lot.

71

Laughing, a thing Sheila hadn't been sure she would know how to do again.

He took her home early and walked her to the door. He politely asked about the possibility of seeing her again, then left.

Sheila was very impressed. He was a gentleman, a fine conversationalist, an excellent dancer, and a very good-looking man. She felt that she had had a very good time despite her fears and nervousness. And he didn't even try to kiss her. Yes, he was a perfect gentleman.

She kept the good feeling with her until she went to bed. There, as she reached to turn off the light, was the picture of Matt and Robin. She returned to the lonely world without the ones she loved so much. As the night passed, so did the feeling as she cried herself to sleep with a prayer to God on her lips.

Sheila had not been out of bed very long the next morning when the phone rang.

"Hello."

"Is this Sheila?"

"Yes."

"I can't talk too loud, they're after me," whispered the voice.

"Who's after you?" inquired Sheila, very perplexed.

"The little men in the white coats. I had such a wonderful time last night, I got back to the hotel and found myself missing your pleasant company. I started to talk to myself and then started asking questions and—"

"Good morning, Earl."

"How did you ever guess?" laughed Earl. "No, really, I did have a wonderful time last night and I did wake up thinking about you this morning. I had a chance to call you to say thanks and to try to talk you into meeting me in the hotel restaurant for lunch at noon today."

"I guess I could." She grinned.

"Fine. See you then."

She hung up the phone and went to sit in the window seat.

What was happening? She felt so good and so anxious, just like a schoolgirl. Maybe this is what she needed after all.

Her thoughts seemed to circle back to yesterday and Earl. Their strange meeting, was it an accident or fate? She wondered if today would bring the same delightful sensations that last night brought?

She sat looking out of the window, daydreaming slightly, as the morning ticked away. She noticed the time and began to get ready.

After a delicious lunch with Earl, she returned home with an invitation for an evening out again. Moments later the doorbell and she received a dozen lovely, red roses from, who else, "the man wearing the white coat and net," alias: Earl.

They found themselves together almost every night that whole week. He never kissed her or made any aggressive advances that would scare her away.

Sheila gained back a little of her self and self-confidence.

He never asked about her past and she never questioned his. They were happy together and that made everything worthwhile.

For the following Sunday, and behind it happy week, a picnic was planned. A picnic. Something else she hadn't done for a very long time.

She felt a great deal of admiration for Earl. He was different.

He picked her up and away they went to the small park just outside of town. A blanket was spread on the ground by the passing river. When they were done eating they lay side by side on the blanket, talking.

"Sheila, you know the past few days have been some that I'll never forget. The kind of days I think about but never see. It makes everything I do worthwhile if I have something to look forward to, with you."

"It's been wonderful for me too, Earl. I've been able to find a reason for living again," she said, looking at the sun-filled sky as she lay on her back.

"I hope I'm, at least, a small part of the reason you feel that way."

"You are. When I'm around you everything is like I'm in a different world. No worries, no haunting memories. Just the beauty of what is here and now.

"You've made me a person again. Don't ask me how or why, you just have.

"To me you're anything but 'just plain,' Earl. You're beginning to be a very special person to me."

"I guess that makes us friends. Or were we ever strangers? Sheila, I think you're a very attractive woman. Even when I met you at the beach and you were feeling so blue and down and out, you were still at your loveliest.

"But it seems lately that you've gained my heart with the many other beauties you possess. The beauty of your smile that makes my day, no matter how shaded it might have been.

"The beauty in your touch that eases all my worries, my frustrations, my fears and doubts. The beauty in your feelings covering the clumsy inconsiderateness that I have a habit of collecting.

"The beauty I hear in your voice that brings aid to a wounded pride, rescues a shattered ego and restores confidence in who I am.

"As Roy Croft once wrote, 'I love you, not for what you are, but for what I am when I'm with you.'

"I think what I'm trying to tell you, Sheila, is that I think I'm falling in love with you."

"I'm flattered that you think you are, but you can't be sure. We've only known each other for such a short time. You know, you haven't even tried to kiss me."

As she spoke, Earl slowly leaned over to Sheila, tenderly placing a kiss on her lips. She closed her eyes and put her arms gently around his neck and kissed him with the great deal of passion that she felt for him.

He looked at her and, ever so gently pushed back the hair

around her face. Tracing her cheek with his finger, he lifted her chin and once again kissed her.

"If I didn't know how wrong I was, I would swear you felt the same way about me."

"Don't ask me to say it right now. Give me a little time, Earl. If it's there, give it time and it will come. It's all happened too fast to be sure. When I'm sure I'll you know and you won't have to question it. It'll be for real."

The sun shone brightly and the river was on its endless way. Birds sang their songs in the towering shade trees and the flowers sent their fragrance on the breeze to enhance the moment. Happiness was being accented and nothing could override it this day.

When I got to my home office, a letter was waiting for me from Sheila. She was confiding in me about her mixed emotions about meeting Earl and asking if she should let it lead anywhere.

Her words were those of one who is in a healing process. who sees the possibilities for life to continue but is afraid to let her feelings surface. Afraid they might bring back painful memories.

I wrote to her with what wisdom I could muster and told her that her heart would dictate her direction when the time was right. Only she would know when the fears would pass. No one could give more sound advice on how to accept things more truthfully and reliably than her own feelings.

I told her I loved her and I knew any decision she would make would be the right one. Little did I know then how those words would come back to haunt me.

Sheila and Earl saw each other almost every day, still as good and close friends, not as lovers. Sheila still had fears about Earl's touching her while the tender thoughts of Matt and her making love were still there. She was not ready to release those moments so fragile and still embossed on her heart.

But not so with those with wagging tongues and vivid imaginations who exploit and manufacture situations through the rumor mill. And as rumor had it. . . .

"Hello, Mrs Stern."

"Oh, hello, Lisa. How are you and your new baby doing?"

"Just fine, thank you."

"What did you name her?"

"Linda. It was my brother Eddy's idea. I don't know where he got the name but my husband and I liked it so much we named her Linda Lynnette," replied Lisa.

"Here comes poor Sheila. I wonder how she's doing?" inquired Mrs. Stern.

"Everybody she can, from what I hear. She sure didn't waste any time to get kissy-faced with that organizer that's staying down at the hotel. I hear she's sleeping with him and making plans," Lisa said sarcastically.

"Are you sure?" questioned Mrs. Stern.

"Yeah, believe it."

"Where did you hear such a thing?"

"Oh . . . it's . . . it's all over town. Well, I have to be going. It was nice talking to you, Mrs. Stern," stammered Lisa, who exited across the street so as not to run into Sheila, who turned into the hotel.

There in the lobby was Earl, making his way to the door.

"I was just on my way over to your house to pick you up. I thought we'd go for a drive, seeing as how hot it is today, and cool off. You know you still haven't shown me around Cedar Dale completely."

"Okay. Your sight-seeing tour guide is at your service," laughed Sheila.

As they left the hotel they passed Mrs. Stern.

"Good afternoon, Mrs. Stern," greeted a cheerful Sheila.

"Sheila," answered Mrs. Stern as she kept on walking.

"A woman of few words," quipped Sheila.

They got into Earl's car and drove endlessly around the town with Sheila pointing out her old high school, the house she and her mother first lived in when they came to Cedar Dale. They were having the time of their lives visiting various sites and trying to stay cool.

The day finally greeted the dusk as the scorching sun sank into the far horizon, as if in answer to the cries for relief from the heat. With the darkening skies a soft summer breeze took hold to give aid and add comfort to the night.

The moon was climbing to its place in the sky, glimmering bright and full as Sheila and Earl came to a stop by the river alongside the old mill.

"What's that?" questioned Earl.

"That's the old mill where they used to bring big cedar trees to be cut a long time ago. That's how the town got its name," explained Sheila.

"What's it used for now?"

"Nothing. Just a hangout for some of the high school kids. It's been condemned but no one pays any attention to it."

"It might make a nice site for an office building for the new company I'm trying to form."

"You might have to ask my brother, Johnny, for permission first," laughed Sheila.

"Your brother? Does he own it? You never mentioned you had a brother."

"Oh, he's not my real brother, but he might as well be. We grew up together. I hear from him from time to time. He's a writer for a major magazine company. He might think ill of you if you took away his 'Shrine of Decisions.' "

"Shrine?"

"Yeah. He says this is a shrine on how people can be so wrong about people. He had a girl in high school that he believed in until he caught her cheating out here the night of our prom when she was supposed to be with him.

"He was really hurt that night and told me that whenever he

77

thinks about trusting his feelings to another girl he'll first think of the shrine and that night."

"Do you think he'll ever find that one girl he can trust some day?"

"Yes. And I want to meet her because she'll be one hell of a woman," grinned Sheila.

They stared into each other's eyes. He slowly put his arm around her and kissed her softly. As she responded to his advances, Earl fumbled for the door latch.

"Let's take a walk," he suggested.

They left the car and, hand in hand, they walked to the river's edge. The swift current passed by unconcerned about the two onlookers as it mirrored the moon's bright beam.

Earl turned to Sheila and put his arms around her and pressed his lips to hers. The more they held each other the more their bodies became aroused.

They slowly lowered their bodies to the soft carpet of grass. They looked into each other's eyes as if each was reading the other's thoughts. Not a word was spoken as they embraced with their bodies straining and beckoning.

Their passion reached an uncontrollable peak, and Sheila, fighting her fears and frustrations, released her restraints and gave herself to Earl.

The heat of the moment was only matched by the heat of the day. A day that Sheila was hoping she would never regret. Or would she?

It was late in the morning when Sheila awoke. She stretched and smiled as if she had the world on a string. She jumped out of bed and got dressed.

Today was to be a special day. She had a feeling, from what Earl had said last night, this might be the day on which she would become a bride-to-be again. She was sure she could make him a good wife and give him all the love that she had in her heart for him.

She hurriedly walked down to his hotel. Walking through the lobby she joyfully nodded and greeted everyone she saw with a smile. She knocked at Earl's door. No answer. Where could he have stepped out to? Maybe he was on the way over to her house. Or maybe he was downtown shopping for that "little important item" he said he was going to give her this day.

She stopped at the front desk on her way out to see if he had told the clerk where was going.

"Did the gentleman in room 212 leave a note where he was going this afternoon?" she questioned.

"Two twelve? Let's see now, 212. I'm afraid the party in room 212 checked out early this morning, miss. I do have a letter left for a Sheila. That you?"

"Yes," answered a very stunned Sheila.

She took the letter and sat down in the lobby and opened it.

My Darling Sheila,

By now you probably realize I have gone. I could not face you to tell you the truth about myself but I tried to hint about this letter last night when I told you I had a "little important item" I wanted to give you today. This is it.

Sheila, there is no way possible I can stop you from hating me. I don't ask it of you, either. Please believe one thing if nothing else, I did love you dearly with every part of my soul. But I have a love of that kind waiting for me back home.

When I arrive there I'm going to try walk in my house and greet my wife and children like I've missed them the whole time I was gone. Like nothing has happened. But down deep inside of me I will live over and over again the joys and happinesses that I had with you.

If I hadn't been married, you would probably be finding yourself with a proposal of marriage on your hands. This is a clumsy sort of a way, but it is my way of telling you that I did love you very much. But we both knew it was just a brief summer interlude and we both must come back to reality.

It will probably be easier for a single girl like you to forget than a married man like myself. You can always find someone else to go out with while I must try to live with it as though it never happened.

I could never leave my wife and children. I imagine a young single girl like you could never realize what life would be like for me without my wife and children.

Sheila, I will admit that I had other affairs before in other towns but you're the only one I ever fell in love with. I know it's hard right now for you to believe me but I meant all those things I told you. You are beautiful and wonderful. You are certainly not one of many but one of few.

Please don't judge me by my actions too harshly. We both had fun, but it's all over and time to put our feet back on the ground.

Stay always the lovely girl you are and someday you'll meet a nice single guy and get married and have a bunch of kids yourself. Then you won't even remember my name. Take care, my love.

With love, Earl.

Sheila's eyes began to fill with tears and pain. Again life had played and toyed with her emotions. She very slowly arose from the chair and walked out of the hotel.

All the way back home she kept remembering the many things they had together. The leaves on the trees were slowly falling to the ground below and a soft breeze stirred them into a colorful mixture of autumn colors. Leaves that held on all through their summer days were now leaving their nurturing security, separating to wither away. Busy people raked and burned them along the curbs and the smoke scented the air. But it was all unnoticed by Sheila as she moved mechanically along the sidewalk toward home. Home, an empty house that again housed an empty shell of a girl who just a few hours before had been ready to lay claim to another crack at happiness. Happiness that was now denied.

The world she thought she had on string turned out to be a yo-yo. And it only brought back more pain and heartache.

16

As weeks passed by, Sheila grew depressed and uncertain again, entering her tomb of fear and anger. Her feelings toward men, any man, were of mistrust and betrayal.

Maybe there wasn't to be another love in her life. Maybe God only allows us one true love in life and hers was used up. *No, that just couldn't be,* she thought to herself. *God must have someone out there who needs me as much as I need him. There's got to be.*

The sun cut through the brisk fall air as Sheila walked to the nearby market to pick up needed items for her evening meal. As she walked up the center aisle of the market she overheard a familiar voice in the next aisle.

"You know, I never would have thought that about Sheila. I always thought she was so sweet and pleasant. I guess when you've been through what she's been through you probably would let go of what moral upbringing you've had, too."

"Yeah, I know what you mean. I knew her mother and although she didn't have a father figure to look up to, I always thought she was a sweet, level-headed type of girl."

"From what I hear, she still looks up to men. . . . from her back." The two laughed. Their voices faded away as they continued down the aisle.

Sheila stood, stunned by what she had heard. As if in a daze, she headed for the checkout stand only to see Lisa and Mrs. Stern turning the corner of the aisle where the voices came from. They never noticed as she left the store upset and tears began to cloud her eyes.

How could they say or believe that about her? Didn't they have anything else to do but blow a fragile situation out of proportion? But in a small town, gossip flows as fast as the river and is as hard to control

What did she do that was so wrong? She knew that Lisa didn't like her very well. She had always blamed Sheila for snubbing her brother Eddy back in high school. But that's when she only had eyes for Matt. What possessed Lisa to take out her vengeance now by telling all these lies?

Sheila tried to wipe her eyes while leaning against a corner of a building. Looking up she saw Buff Taylor coming down the sidewalk. Not wanting to explain to him why she was crying, she darted through the nearest doorway.

As her eyes adjusted to the darkened room from the bright light outside, she found herself in a small bar. Only three people occupied separate seats at the bar. She made her way to an empty booth and sat down.

The bartender came over to the booth, his shirt unbuttoned halfway down the front. He wore a soiled apron, which he was drying his hands on. He looked at Sheila and smiled.

"What ya need, hon?"

"Oh . . . ah . . . a beer, I guess," stammered Sheila, uncertain and still somewhat shaken. She opened her purse to search for money as the bartender approached and set the beer down.

"The gentleman at the end of the bar paid for it."

Sheila looked over to the end of the bar. A middle-aged man smiled and nodded. She was sure she had never seen him before. When she glanced back again, she noticed him walking over to her.

"Hi. My name is Don."

"Thank you for the beer. Mine's Sheila."

"Ya, I know. A couple of friends of mine pointed you out one day and I never forget a pretty face. I do a little traveling for my company. I come through here every couple of months and I thought you and I could get together, have a few beers, and go over to my motel for a while," he said with a Cheshire-cat grin.

"And why would I want to do that?" Sheila answered coyly.

"You know, party a little. Have some fun. I think I can handle your price."

"I don't know who you've been talking to, but buddy, you could never handle my price! Now get the hell out of my sight before I scream bloody murder."

"Who are you trying to fool? Half the people I do business with say you're an easy mark. Why pick me out to get sore at?"

"I said get lost! Or I'll . . . "

"Or you'll what?" he grinned.

"Or she'll call me and I'll have to throw your sorry ass into jail and throw away the key," came a robust voice from behind Sheila. It was Sheriff Taylor. His eyes were fixed and glaring at the salesman.

Upon seeing his badge shining off one of the dim lights, he jumped up and left the bar.

"Thank you, Buff," sighed Sheila.

"My pleasure. I thought I saw you come in here but I wasn't sure. I've never seen you go into a place like this unescorted before. Sheila, is there anything wrong? You know you can come to me if there is."

"Oh, Buff, I just don't know. I overheard some people gossiping today and found out I was the main topic of conversation around here. Now this. What did I do that was so wrong?"

"Nothing. You got your heart broken and a few gossips see their own fantasies in it. And that is what they talk about. Sheila, consider the source of some of these rumors and just disregard them. Not everybody listens to rumors you know," Buff explained.

They got up from the booth and Buff walked Sheila home. Again, Sheila took up residence in her window seat, looking for answers. She watched as the late fall skies began to cloud over. A feeling of despair gripped her emotions with a force she had never known.

If only Matt were here, she thought. *Or Johnny. No, on second thought I would be too ashamed for them to hear the awful rumors.*

She sat alone in frustration and confusion, contemplating where life would now lead her. Should she live a lifestyle of being alone or one of hostility toward the lies that were trying to engulf her? As her thoughts deepened so did the clouds, bringing a gentle, fall rain; the darkness ended another day of heartbreak.

I never knew of Sheila's situation until a few months later when I called Sheriff Taylor.

"Buff, this is Johnny Eastman. I hate to bother you but I'm worried about Sheila. I've called several times and sent letters but I can't seem to reach her. Is she all right?

"Can't rightly say, Johnny. A lot's happened to that girl since you seen her last." Buff then led me through a trail of love, betrayal, heartbreak, and anger. He told me of a girl in self-imposed exile from everyone for a short time. Then, attempting to regain her life, she fell into living out the vicious gossip lifestyle.

He told me of a girl I didn't know. My worst dream had happened. Sheila had turned gossip fantasy into reality. Even worse, Buff didn't know where she had gone.

I had just concluded my current assignment and called the home office for a leave of absence. I left on the first bus out of town but wasn't sure where to start. I was trying to find a girl I now didn't even know. But I realized I must try. I had to find her. I had to help her. But where could she be? *God, please help me,* I pleaded.

My search started in Cedar Dale as I borrowed Buff's car. I reached many dead ends and it seemed like frustration was my only companion.

Then one day, an unexpected conversation caught my ear and attention. I was sitting in a restaurant when, from the next booth, I overheard. . . .

"Don't that beat all. Here I was sitting at this bar and she came right up to me and asked me to buy her a drink. Well, I looked around because the last time I bought her a beer here in this town, the sheriff butted in and scared the living shit right out of me.

"I didn't know they were friends and he was watching over her. So I left as fast as I could. Now she turns up in a bar over in Delridge just as juiced up as she can get. She may call herself Sheila but she screws like the Queen of Sheba," he concluded.

As the two got up to leave I got up, too.

"Pardon me, but did I just hear you mention a girl named Sheila?" I questioned.

"Maybe. What's it to you?"

"Well, I heard a lot about that girl and I'll give you twenty bucks if you can tell me where I could find her."

"Twenty bucks? Well, sure, but I probably partied her out," he laughed. "She was in the Peacock Bar and Grill over in Delridge last time I saw her. How about my twenty?"

"Sure. Here's twenty for the information. And here is a little something from Sheila." I said as my knee came up hard between his legs, sending him backward into the booth. I grabbed my coat and headed for the door and Delridge.

Delridge was only a few miles from Cedar Dale, so I reached there as the red fall sun was barely touching the tops of the trees as it fell into the horizon. I located the Peacock and grabbed a booth and a beer.

The night grew long and I thought I wouldn't find her this night. As I was about to get up and leave, low and behold, the door opened and Sheila and another woman came in with a man in the middle holding onto both ladies' arms.

He sat them down at a table and pointed at them like a master telling his dogs to stay. He walked to the bar and mingled with a couple of gentlemen in business suits. He nodded over to Sheila and the other woman and the men looked at them.

I watched him return to the table and talk to the two women. I saw Sheila shake her head, "no." He quickly grabbed her arm and spoke to her again. She nodded, then he walked back up to the bar.

The one man started to go for his wallet, but Sheila's friend caught his arm and he put it back in his pocket.

He was pimping. He was selling Sheila. The two at the bar got up off the stools and followed him into the men's restroom. This was my chance.

I hurriedly got up and went to the table where the two women were sitting. As I approached she looked up all glassy-eyed and disoriented.

"Johnny?" she said.

I grabbed her and headed for the door. I pushed Sheila through it and looked back as the three men were coming out of the restroom. I hastened her into my car and rushed to the driver's side. As I drove away I could see the three men exiting the bar, looking in every direction. But I had Sheila.

I turned to her. She was weeping and mumbling over and over: "I'm sorry, Johnny. I'm sorry, Johnny."

I slowed the car down from my getaway speed and put my arm up as Sheila moved to the shelter and protection of it.

"Don't hate me, Johnny. I don't know what happened. Just don't hate me."

"Sheila, I don't hate you. I love you. If I didn't I wouldn't be here right now. You mean the whole world to me and as long as I'm alive I'll watch over you, little sister."

Sheila laid her head on my shoulder as her arms wrapped around my waist. She cried and I smiled as we drove back toward Cedar Dale, where the tongues were hot and the welcome cold. Could we temper our patience and find forgiving to forge a new beginning for Sheila? Or would we stir up the embers of a living hell?

17

As I prepared to leave Cedar Dale, I felt I had covered all my bases for right now. I got Sheila an apartment to stay in since she had lost her house while she was away. Buff assured me he would watch over Sheila and let me know if anything happened so I could return to help, if necessary.

She had seemed to take a liking to an older couple who had five kids and were expecting another in a couple of months. Pat and Howard seemed like very sensible people who did not heed gossip or worry about a person's past.

We had also run into Eddy Pratt, a one-time friend, who had had a crush on Sheila back in our high-school days. I knew Eddy would stick up for Sheila no matter what. Even against his sister, Lisa, who started so many lies about Sheila. He was impressionable and naive, but honest and loyal to the core.

I felt I was comfortable with everything, so I returned to my home office for reassignment. I caught the next bus out, but my mind was still on Sheila.

"Sheila, this is Eddy," came the greeting through the phone. "I was hoping I could take you out for a burger and a movie tonight."

"I'm sorry Eddy, but Pat and Howard have asked me out to their farm for dinner."

"Oh. Well, maybe another time, then," came the clearly disappointed voice.

"Well, they asked me out to dinner but I could go to the late show if you want."

"Yeah, okay! I mean, that would be great. Do you want me to pick you up at Howard's? I know where they live."

"Does eight o'clock sound okay?"

"Super. I'll be there," answered Eddy with a noticeable change in his voice.

Sheila hung up the phone as a car horn blared from the driveway. It was Howard. He drove her to their farm just outside of town. When they arrived, Pat was in the kitchen with two of mommy's little helpers, while the rest gathered in the front room with their coloring books.

"Can I help?" Sheila inquired.

"No, it's just about done. Go in the front room and sit a spell."

Sheila felt strange and yet good being around the children. It was basically the first time she'd been around kids since Robin died. It was a good feeling. It was a warm and comfortable feeling. She felt a bit envious of this environment, which she never got to have because of the loss of Matt and Robin.

After dinner was over, Sheila returned to the front room to play with the children until Eddy arrived. At the second stroke of eight there came a knock on the door from a very eager Eddy.

There were many more movies for Sheila and Eddy in the next few weeks. They spent a great deal of time together. Sheila got a job as a waitress at the local café. Eddy spent a good portion of her shift just hanging around.

Eddy tried a few times to let Sheila know how serious he was about her. Sheila was still in a fragile state when it came to men but felt relaxed around Eddy, knowing how trustworthy and reliable he was. She also didn't take Eddy's declarations of love for her that seriously.

There were times he would bring down Linda, Lisa's little girl, to the café and the three of them would split a milkshake together. They had their laughter and fun together. Many times Sheila caught herself staring at Linda and wondering about Robin.

December came, the winter snow came, and Pat and Howard's little bundle from heaven came. Sheila had been helping out by taking care of the other children right up to the time Pat had the baby. She was almost as thrilled as Pat when the baby was born.

While Pat was in the hospital, Sheila cooked and washed for the family whenever she was needed. Eddy would take her out to the farm and Howard would bring her to work.

When Eddy entered the café that day his step had a little spring to it. This was going to be a big day for him. His eyes searched for Sheila but he didn't see her anywhere.

"Who ya looking for Eddy?" called out one of the fellows at the café.

"Sheila. She should be here by now. She didn't call in sick or anything, did she?"

"I don't think so. She'll probably be here in a minute," reassured the gentleman.

The young kid on the stool next to him bumped his friend's arm and said in a low whisper, "Watch this. Eddy's a sucker for a story." He turned around to Eddy.

"Say Eddy, I don't want to butt in or anything but ah . . . are you going to let that Sheila make a sap out you?"

"What do you mean?"

"Well now, no offense to you, but she went with Howard out to his place. Now there might not be anything wrong, but you remember how they say Sheila used to be. I've heard tell that Howard has mentioned how he would like to get into her pants. His wife, I hear, is still in the hospital after having that new baby and I was thinking. . . . "

"No!" exclaimed Eddy. "No, Sheila isn't like that anymore. She's a wonderful, lovable good woman now. I'd appreciate you not going around saying things that aren't true. She's been out there watching their kids."

"Sorry, I just thought I'd mention it."

"You don't know Sheila as well as I do. She would never do

that," repeated Eddy, trying to toss away the seed of doubt that had been planted in his mind.

"If he doesn't believe me," mumbled the youth, turning his back to Eddy and winking to his grinning friend, "all he has to do is check with Tim."

Hearing every word he turned to the owner at the other end of the counter.

"Tim, where's Sheila tonight? Did she call in and say she'd be late or something?"

"No, Eddy. Howard came up and picked her up and they drove out to his farm. She said if you came in to tell you she'd be back in just a little while and to just wait for her."

"Oh!" exclaimed Eddy, a little bewildered. "Well, I, ah . . . have to ah . . . pick up something I left at home. Tell her I'll be right back."

Eddy left the café without the spring in his step he had earlier. Once outside, he leaned up against his car and tried to talk himself out of the doubt he had.

Meanwhile, out at the farmhouse, Howard opened the door and he and Sheila entered. Howard looked at her.

"Sheila, Pat and I sure want to thank you for all the help you've given us. With me gone a good share of the time and her in her past condition you just don't know how much worry you've saved us."

"Howard, you and Pat know I'd do just about anything for you. You two have been the only ones, outside of Eddy, that have had faith in me and tried to help me forget the past. I'd do a great deal just to repay your kindness."

"Hell, we figure a person is good until they prove different to us."

"Well, anyway, thanks," said Sheila. "But now let's hurry and get those clothes packed so you can take them up to Pat. Besides, I have to get back to work and be there when Eddy shows up."

"You think a lot of this Eddy guy, don't you?" inquired Howard.

"I don't know. You know me. I just can't convince myself that

90

he means everything that he says. I've learned to be cautious by getting hurt so much. I do think I might even love the guy if I would let myself."

Sheila continued to walk back and forth with Howard as she packed the hospital-bound suitcase. As she did, she came upon a very sheer nightgown. Admiring it for a short time, Howard walked in and saw her smiling.

"Want it? It's yours."

"What? Oh no, I couldn't. What would Pat say?"

"She wouldn't care. In fact, she'd probably want you to have it. Besides, every time I saw her in it I got batty. Then I got shook and she got pregnant again. Please take it. After all, six kids is a little too much overtime for that devil garment," he chuckled.

They laughed aloud and then Sheila gave him a friendly kiss. But the eyes that peer and never hear, often misinterpret. So was it with the eyes staring from the driveway of the farm.

Eddy's heart felt a great pain and the muscles in his stomach seem to be tied in a knot. He figured he had seen enough. All he wanted to do now was to get out of there. As he started up his motor, the two innocent victims of circumstances looked out the window.

"Isn't that Eddy's car?" asked Howard.

"Yes, but . . . I hope he didn't get the wrong idea about that kiss. Howard, let's go and catch him. I have to explain," cried Sheila as she picked up her coat.

When they jumped into the car they could see Eddy turning down the snow-covered gravel road. Howard floored his pedal and out the drive they went. They followed him up and down graveled roads until they finally appeared to be gaining on him. Then . . . nothing.

"Where did he go? Have we lost him?" cried Sheila.

"No, the little fool turned off his headlights. He could get himself killed that way."

Their eyes searched the night as they slowed down slightly trying to guess which tire tracks in the snow were Eddy's. Suddenly there appeared a glare in the sky. The line of evergreens gave way to clear vision and they saw it.

Sheila put her hand to her mouth in fright.

"Oh my God!" shouted Howard. "He's missed the 'T' intersection."

As they approached the burning auto, Sheila jumped out of the car.

"God, Howard, get him out. Get him out. Please hurry, please," shouted Sheila, panic stricken.

Howard quickly jumped out of the car and down into the ditch. Rolling in the snow and scooping up a handful he reached for the door handle. The snow sizzled against the hot metal as flames licked at his arm. Pulling open the door, his eyes scanned the inside, but no Eddy. Then he noticed the broken side window and a figure lying out in the snow on the other side of the car. Rushing over to him was Sheila.

"Howard, over here."

"Yeah, I see. I'm coming."

Sheila knelt down in the snow and placed his head on her lap.

"I'm going to call for an ambulance. Will you be all right until I get back?"

Sheila nodded her head. Howard rushed back to the car and sped away. Looking down at Eddy's dirty, blood-covered face, she took out her handkerchief and started to wipe away the blood that was running down from a cut at the hairline.

"Why, Sheila? Why?" whispered Eddy, with his eyes half-opened.

"Oh, Eddy. Hush, I'll explain later. Howard's gone for an ambulance."

"No need," coughed Eddy. His hand that held his sports jacket loosened and Sheila bit on her hand to keep from yelling. He revealed an incision across his stomach that was as neatly cut as if done by a surgeon's own hand.

"I guess . . . that'll teach me not . . . to go through car windows while they're still up." Eddy tried to smile but the grimace of pain kept a firm grip on him.

"Sheila, this was . . . to be the most wonderful night of my life. I love you, you know." His eyes strained to remain open, like a person fighting sleep, and his coughing continued. "I was even going to prove it with this. . . . "

As his hand barely entered the pocket of his jacket his words stopped, his coughing stopped, and his stiffness relaxed.

"Eddy? Eddy? Oh, God, not you, too, Eddy. Oh, God no!" cried Sheila. Her tears were falling on his cold face washing the blood and dirt away. She brushed the tears from her eyes and continued the interrupted entry into his pocket. She pulled out a little white box. It dropped from her hand as she tried to open it. As it fell to the snow it opened and Sheila's face turned to stone.

There in the snow, collecting all the brilliance from the flaming car, was a small diamond ring. She picked it up and brushed the snow off it then placed it on her finger. Slowly she took off her coat and placed it under his head. She looked at the silent figure that was once a man.

"Oh, my dear Eddy. My precious Eddy. I love you, too," whispered Sheila as she gently placed a kiss on his lips.

Sheila then stood up slowly. With the stare of a blindman she walked up to the wire fence surrounding a field of white emptiness and climbed through. Slowly she walked off into the snow-covered field as the cold night winds lashed at her dress sleeves. She didn't even hear the small screaming sirens approaching off in the distance.

The winds seemed to heed her feelings as they swept the loose, fallen snow over her tracks as if she had never passed that way before.

18

I had no idea how urgent Buff Taylor's message was that dragged me away from my assignment. He found out from my home office that I was just a few miles away from Cedar Dale and wired me. I had planned to stop by the old stomping grounds to see Sheila and some of my friends when I had finished this story. But Buff's wire insisted that I leave now.

As I entered his office in Cedar Dale I felt things weren't just right.

"Johnny," said Buff, as he got up to shake my hand. "Johnny, I sure am glad you could come."

"Your wire said it was urgent. I hope you exaggerated, Buff."

"I'm afraid not. Johnny, a few weeks ago we had a pretty bad accident around here. Eddy Pratt was killed."

"Eddy? I'm sorry to hear about it, of course, but what does his death have to with me?"

I sat down in the chair in front of his desk as Buff went to the window and looked out.

"Did you know Eddy was seeing Sheila?"

"Not really. He was a sensible guy. I'd say she had good taste."

"Then you didn't know that he was going to ask her to marry him?"

"No. What are you getting at, Buff?"

"Johnny, we've been good friends for quite some time. We both have tried to help Sheila all we could. I know you have her good interests at heart more than any one ever did. Now when she needs someone, my hands are tied here in the office."

"What are you trying to tell me? She hasn't left again, has she?"

"I'm afraid so. The same night Eddy got killed. She was the last one to see him alive and no one has seen her since. I got worried about what she might do under the circumstances. Let me explain what happened."

As Buff explained I knew why he had sent for me so abruptly. I had to go and find Sheila. I didn't know where to start, exactly. The only thing that kept going through my mind was my hope she hadn't gone back to the bottle and hustling as a means of running away from reality, like she had the last time. I couldn't let anything happen to my little Sheila.

I left Cedar Dale on a hunch that I might know where Sheila had gone. I hopped a bus to where I had found her the last time. I was hoping she had not retreated back to her old ways, but I was uncertain just how hard she would take the pain of losing, again, someone she loved.

When we pulled into the bus depot I quickly emerged from the bus and went straight to the same dive I'd scraped her out of the last time. I walked through the doors and up to the bar. The smoke was so thick it was enough to choke me. The small group at the bar gave me the once-over as I ordered a drink. I had barely gotten my drink in my hand when a girl came over and sat down beside me.

"Hi," she said. "Would you like to buy me a drink?"

Just then another woman approached us.

"Beat it, Sue. I know this guy."

It was the woman that was with Sheila last time I was here. I felt my luck was holding on.

"Yeah, looking for Sheila?"

"Is she here?"

"No. At least not now. She came in a few days back all blank faced like a zombie or something, with no coat, no purse, no nothing. She was half sick. I don't ever remembering seeing her that bad. Even before, when we had a bad night or a john that was a little extra rough or mean, we looked bad the next morning. But she never was as bad as she was when she came in this time."

"Where'd she go? She's been hurt bad and I must get to her before she does something stupid."

"She didn't seem to be hurt any place when she was in here."

"Not physically. Mentally. She blames herself for a man's death, which was not her fault."

"The kid is pretty well mixed-up then, isn't she? I guess that's why she agreed so easily to go south with Denny. Ya know, even as bad as she drank and as depressed as she got, she still never wanted anything to do with him and here she said yes to him the first time he asked."

"South? Where south? Did he mention any town or state or anything? I have to know," I questioned with an urgency in my voice.

"He didn't have to. Everyone knows he's out of Tampa, Florida. That's where you'll find him. Just ask for Denny Troy, at any bar."

"Is he a barfly?"

"No. He's a pimp."

I felt deflated inside in realizing that things were worse then I had first feared. I thanked her for the information and headed back to the bus station to find out when the next bus left for Tampa.

Soon I was on my way again. I didn't know where in Tampa to start or what to expect when and if I found her. It took me almost three days before I reached Tampa. I had always wanted to go down there on a visit, but not one of this kind.

I grabbed a sandwich and started my rounds of the bars. I must have spent four days or more going from one bar to another. Some admitted they knew Denny Troy, but no one knew when he'd be in or where to get in touch with him.

The only ray of hope I received was one night when I got myself invited to an after-hours club. One of the local crowd made mention that he had seen Denny the day before there. But like the rest he knew nothing about getting hold of him. At least I knew he was in town.

It was one month to the day since I had left Cedar Dale and I felt no closer now than I did then. My main worry was how the last two months since the accident had affected Sheila. If she was still in Tampa why couldn't I find her?

I guess I still had a little luck with me the day I ate by the window of that small café. For it was there I noticed the lights flashing off and on across the street at an obscure little lounge I had overlooked before in my search. I finished and walked over to it.

The music was loud and live. The bar was near the door. I headed for it as I looked over the assorted patrons sitting at the bar, at the tables, in the booths, and those standing. Many of the women sat alone at tables near the front entrance. I asked for Denny Troy.

"Denny Troy? I don't see him right now but he should be back," said the lovely young bartender.

"Could you tell me if he has been in with a young lady with blonde hair?"

"Denny always comes in with someone different and most of the women aren't ladies."

I sat there feeling that my search might be close to its climax. I asked for change for cigarettes and made my way through the crowd to the machine.

As I turned around a woman bumped into me. She could hardly hold her balance as drunk as she was. Her make-up was on too thick and very much over-accented. I thought to myself that from what I had seen she was typical of this crowd.

Maybe Sheila won't be here I didn't think even she would lower herself to this level. I finally made my way back up to the bar and my drink.

Suddenly a commotion started a few tables away. It was the drunken girl and some guy. He was slapping her silly while everyone just sat there. The girl behind the bar tapped me on the shoulder.

"That's Denny Troy."

I started to get up just as I noticed that the girl's hair had come undone from the high hairdo she had and fallen down past her shoulders like Sheila's. Without giving it another thought I realized the drunk I had run into was Sheila. I had not even recognized her with all the make-up on.

I quickly ran over and turned Denny Troy around and let go with all I had. He went headlong into a couple of tables. He picked himself up slowly and I grabbed a hold of Sheila's hand.

"Sheila, are you all right?"

She slowly lifted her head. Blood was running down the side of her mouth and tears melted the heavy mascara.

"Johnny? Johnny?" she whispered, reaching out to touch my face.

Just then I saw Denny picking up a bottle, out of the corner of my eye. I turned swiftly.

"You punk. You lousy punk," he yelled as he broke the bottle across the edge of the table.

He lunged at me like a soldier with a bayonet. I dodged his thrust and grabbed his arm as I came up with my knee into his midsection. He dropped the broken bottleneck and I knocked him backward onto the floor.

I once again reached for Sheila. She barely had enough strength to lift herself out of the chair she was in. We started for the door when I heard someone scream. I turned and noticed he was holding a knife.

As he started toward me I pushed Sheila to one side. He was halfway to me when a figure came from out of the crowd and brought a small revolver to the back of his head. It was the manager. He told us to go and he'd take care of everything. We called for a cab and we went back to my hotel.

Sheila could hardly hold herself up while I fumbled to get the hotel door open. Quickly, I turned on the lights and guided Sheila inside. She sat down on the bed and stared aimlessly at the floor.

"Johnny, why do you bother with scum like me?"

I looked at her and grinned as I reached for the phone.

"Well, what's a big brother for if he doesn't care what happens to his kid sister?"

"Oh, Johnny. I feel so sick inside. I think I need a drink. Just one drink, Johnny, and I'll be okay."

I hung up the phone after ordering a hot pot of coffee from room service. Looking through the drawers proved hopeless as to finding something for Sheila to sleep in.

"What ya lookin' for, Johnny?" inquired Sheila, as she wove back and forth on the bed.

"A nightgown, pajamas, or something for you to sleep in."

"Oh, that's all right. I'll just sleep in what I usually sleep in."

A knock came at the door. I answered it.

"Room service. Did you order some coffee?"

"Yes," I said, digging in my pocket for some change for a tip. As I looked back up at the bellhop, I noticed his interests were more inside the room. Looking around behind me, I saw Sheila, standing as naked as the day. I quickly shut the door.

"Sheila!"

"Well, this is what I usually sleep in," she said as she climbed in between the covers. "Oh, Johnny, I don't feel so good. Don't leave, will you?"

"I'm right here, babe. Now try to drink some of this coffee." As I spoke, her hand relaxed and her eyes completed their closing.

"Well, maybe you deserve to pass out," I chuckled. "You little fool, what am I going to do with you? You can't keep running off to this kind of life every time you get hurt.

"My Sheila, my poor, little Sheila. Maybe you have suffered more than your share of pain but I can't stand by and let the girl I once knew and the girl I love so . . . that slipped out I guess. Down deep I guess I do love you in my own way.

"We've been through so much together. I guess we've experienced more than a great many married couples ever do in a lifetime.

"You little nut, look at yourself," I continued as I touched my

99

finger to the side of her cheek. "Make-up on so thick it hides the young beauty which is yours. It makes you look old before your time. And your hair. Fitting only for lice or a bird's nest. It's not the same hair that once hung down so long and well-brushed, the hair that accented the beautiful young lady you once were and still are.

"Sheila, oh, Sheila, this isn't you. This is the mockery of yourself in your hurt and twisted mind. I do care very much what happens to you. I guess . . . I guess maybe I do love you, but you'll never know it. It wouldn't be fair to you. As far as you're concerned, I'm just a friend."

Just then Sheila tossed and turned calling out, "Johnny! Johnny!" She screamed.

"I'm right here, Sheila. Right here. Everything's okay."

I placed my hand on hers. She held it to her breasts and squeezed it with both her hands. I smiled as I pushed back the fallen hair from across her face with my other hand. Carefully I slipped my hand out and went into the bathroom to get a damp washcloth. I very tenderly started to wipe off some of the coated make-up she had on.

Drinking coffee and smoking cigarettes, I sat alongside the bed in the dark. Thinking and debating, I stared at Sheila's outline in the dark as one would study a work of art. The only time she would move was when she would toss and turn, calling out names from her past, the past that haunted her as a nightmare of fear.

It was with much relief that I watched the dawn rise and a more sound sleep possessed Sheila. I was so relieved that I also drifted off into a peaceful sleep.

As I awoke I quickly glanced over at Sheila. She was lying there smiling with tears in her eyes.

"What's the matter?" I asked, leaving the chair and sitting on the edge of the bed. "What's wrong?"

"Nothing. I just feel like at times I have a guardian angel who watches over me. Then I open my eyes and you're always there. When I need you the most, you're always there. Then I got to thinking. What if someday I opened my eyes and you weren't there? Oh, Johnny, never leave me. I'm afraid someday I'll never see you again. I don't think I could live with that."

I looked into her eyes, eyes that held tears, pain, and now fear. They were helplessly calling out for someone to care. We sat there looking into each other's eyes. I brushed my hand across her cheek. She lifted her arms and placed them around my neck as I leaned down to place a gentle kiss on her lips. Pulling me down to her, Sheila pressed her lips firmly to mine.

"Johnny, why couldn't you have love me as more than just a sister?"

I pulled back slightly and whispered in her ear. "I do love you, Sheila. I guess down deep I've always loved you, for a very long time."

"Oh, Johnny, I love you, too. So very much I do."

We kept our embrace as Sheila cried. Only this time her tears were tears of joy, not pain. I turned my head toward the window and then back to Sheila.

"Looks like it's going to be a lovely day," I said, smiling.

"A very lovely day," she answered, wiping the tears off her radiant smile.

"Honey, are you very sure you're in love with me?" I questioned.

"Yes, but why . . . "

"Sheila, will you marry me? Don't think about it, just answer."

"Well ah . . . ah . . . yes, I guess. . . . But, Johnny, where could we ever go that someone wouldn't someday come up to you and say, 'Hey Mac, did you ever know I took your wife to bed?' Where could we ever live without gossip about me? Maybe you're asking for a bad bargain."

"We're going to live in Cedar Dale."

"Cedar Dale! You're nuts," exclaimed Sheila.

"No, I'm not. We're going to be married there, live there, and raise a family there. And we're going to do it all on Bloomgarden Avenue. We'll make them eat crow."

"On Bloomgarden Avenue! You are nuts."

"We'll have the respect we're entitled to or a few people are going to end up as human interest subjects in the magazine I work for."

"Now I know you're nuts. Why . . . why . . . why, that's almost blackmail."

"Yeah, I know," I grinned.

We laughed from deep inside, from a place that had been used previously only as a hideaway for pain. We embraced and kissed. We talked of love and made love. For today the world was ours. Let no man tread on our dreams this day.

19

Sheila and I spent a few more days in Tampa sunning ourselves on the sandy beaches and trying to get some lost color back into Sheila's skin. We had fun together and found that we did enjoy each other and that love was truly ours. I believe she smiled more in that short time then she probably had in all the last months.

But, like all good things, we had to pack up and leave and end this dream that we found. I guess we didn't take it too badly, realizing that we were going to have the rest of our lives together.

I still had to finish the story I was on for my magazine. I had left it unfinished in my search for Sheila and now it had to be completed. So Sheila, with all her little fears, and me with all my high hopes, left the sun and sand and traveled back north to Cedar Dale.

The first few days we were back tongues were prepared to wag, but many of the people were basically good and were willing to wait and watch before passing judgment.

At first I went everyplace Sheila went, just to be there if someone would speak out against her. Then I could stand up and speak on Sheila's behalf. It seemed only one person insisted on keeping the flame of the past burning. It was Eddy's sister, Lisa.

Lisa still blamed Sheila for Eddy's death and consistently spread rumors about her since her affair with Earl. It seems she thought she was a better judge of character then even her brother. I knew better.

If she had had better taste in high school she wouldn't have been labeled by everyone in school as a pick-up party playmate.

When she had to get married, her family tried to keep it pretty much a secret so as not to disgrace their good name and position on Bloomgarden Avenue. Ever since, she'd been an agitator.

I spent a week with Sheila in Cedar Dale before I wired my home office that I was returning to finish my last assignment. I was just a short ways from Cedar Dale so I borrowed the use of Buff Taylor's car. He'd been a true friend through all of this and I was very grateful.

We made the final move to keep the telltale tongues silent. Just before I left we made the announcement of our marriage plans. I even put a down payment on a house on Bloomgarden Avenue like I told Sheila I would. I still remember that happy, blank expression she had on her face when I told her. When I was completely satisfied that everything was okay, I left for a few days to complete my story.

I called back many times to check on everything. I guess, to be truthful, I called just to hear Sheila's voice because I missed her so. She sounded so happy and nothing like the girl I'd found two weeks ago. She was really happy for the first time in a long time and that made all my temples, inside me.

She said she missed me. It was the first time in many a year that I felt the warmth and caring of someone reaching out to me. It was a good feeling.

Back in Cedar Dale, Sheila was a busy young lady, preparing for my return and our wedding day. With her arms loaded down with packages, Sheila made her way down Bloomgarden Avenue. Her smile gave off a warmth that radiated from her heart.

Now she knew I was right. The townspeople hardly said a word about her anymore. She didn't know if it was because of me or because they were hoping she would become the girl they once knew. Either way they weren't talking and hurting me and that's all that really mattered to her. If only Lisa would feel the same way and forgive her.

"Hello, Mrs. Beck," smiled Sheila as she approached her at the corner.

"Oh, hello, Sheila. My, what a load of packages. Getting ready for the wedding I see."

"Yes. I can hardly wait for the next three days to pass. Of course, the past few days passed quite rapidly up till now. I'm trying to get the house that Johnny bought ready for us to move into."

"When will Johnny be back?"

"Today. In fact, any minute now. If you'll excuse me I'll be running along. I still have to get dressed and ready. I don't want him to think he's marrying a witch," Sheila chuckled as she crossed the street.

Halfway down the block she saw Lisa's daughter Linda playing. She remembered what fun they had had when Eddy used to bring her to the café and other times when they went to movies.

"Hi, Linda."

"Hi, Sheila," Linda said, smiling. "Gee, I haven't seen you for a gosh-awful long time."

As Linda started to go toward Sheila, Lisa stepped out of her house. Noticing right away what was taking place across the street, she called to her daughter.

"Linda! Come home. Right now. Come on."

"Oh, okay," she responded, a little disappointed.

"Right now. Get over here!" persisted Lisa.

Linda began to walk with her head down. She did not check for the oncoming traffic. She had no more than gotten off the curb when a car turned the corner. Sheila saw the car coming and that it was making no effort to slow down. She looked back at Linda.

Suddenly all Sheila could see was Robin. Robin running out in front of the car. Her little Robin. This time, she must save Robin! Dropping her packages, she darted toward Linda.

"Robin, look out! A car! Look out!"

Lisa also saw the oncoming, speeding car heading for her child. She let out a harsh and loud scream.

"No, Robin, not again! I'll save you, my little darling," muttered Sheila, who ran as fast as her legs would carry her. "Mommy won't fail you this time."

When she reached Linda she gave a hard push. Then came a screech of tires skidding along the pavement and a final thud. The woman rushed out of the car as Lisa ran for her daughter.

"Don't touch her. Call an ambulance," cried Mrs. Beck as she ran down the street.

I stopped my car at the stop sign as I saw Mrs. Beck calling to me.

"Johnny, quick. Sheila's been hurt."

I exploded out of my car and ran to the accident. When I got there, there lay Sheila, limp, with blood running across her face, her dress torn.

"Sheila! Sheila! Oh, my God. What happened? What happened?"

"Johnny," spoke Lisa, "she saved Linda's life. She pushed her out of the way of the car and saved her life."

"Johnny. Johnny," whispered Sheila.

"Right here, honey," I said, kneeling down.

"Johnny, hold me. I'm so scared. Hold me, please."

I took her gently into my trembling arms.

"Oh, Johnny. I hope this doesn't delay our wedding."

"No. There is nothing that can keep us from getting married. You're not getting away from me that easy, young lady. I'll even push you down the aisle in a wheelchair if I have to." I tried to force a grin through my tears.

My heart was breaking as I wiped off the blood and dirt from her pretty face. The neighborhood gathered around us, but I could only see my precious Sheila.

"Johnny, I love you. You know I love you, don't you?"

"Yes, Sheila, I know. And I love you with all my heart and soul."

"I don't look very pretty for your homecoming, do I?"

"Honey, you're always beautiful to me. You look all right, just all right. Now relax."

"I saved Robin, darling. Now Matt doesn't have to go away. She is safe, isn't she, Johnny?"

"Yes, Sheila. Robin's safe, now relax."

"My Johnny, my darling Johnny. Are you sure I can marry my brother?" she asked trying to show a smile.

"No trouble," I grinned.

"Johnny?"

"What, my darling?"

"Johnny, kiss me. Please kiss me and tell me again, please."

"I love you, Sheila," I said holding back my tears. My lips tenderly caressed hers. I felt my heart crumble as I felt her body go limp in my arms. The arms that held her with so much love now became her haven for death.

"Sure is a terrible way to die for a girl like her," I heard someone say in the crowd.

"Her kind always ends up that way," came the reply.

"You lousy hypocrites!" I shouted as I came to my feet and spun around. "You ungrateful, lousy hypocrites. What kind of a girl do you think she was? What kind of a girl have you made her and driven her to be? My guts are so knotted with the stink in this town that if I could vomit it would be the first clean thought that's been on this block for years. You're the first ones to make notes of someone's misgivings but you're the last ones to reach out and give aid when it's needed.

"You've all known me and you've all known Sheila. Yet, you say I was a little better than her. But it was only because you haven't had me at the end of your waggling tongues. This girl here was and is better than any one of you.

"She never had a bad thought about you. She never spread one goddamn rumor about you, although she could have. She never drove you out of your hometown with vicious lies and immoral prejudices.

"What was she? You treated her like a weed that infiltrated a patch of puritan flowers. If you ask me, she was a rose surviving among a batch of bitch thistles.

"She grew up on this street just like you and me. She didn't want to be treated like a queen, although to me and a few others, she was. All she wanted was to live here without your wagging tongues lashing out at her.

"Johnny, I . . . " started Lisa.

"And you, Lisa. You the pure. How far back do you want me to dig up your past? High school, maybe? You know what I mean, don't you, Lisa? Yet, you keep saying that Sheila wasn't good enough for your brother Eddy. Well, maybe she just wasn't good enough to sacrifice her life for your child. But here she lies. And knowing Sheila, she probably would do it again. Maybe if you look close enough you can find some fault in that, too. I'm certain you'll try." I hung my head for a moment. There was a complete silence.

"You know, at one time I was very proud to answer the question 'where ya from buddy?' But now I abhor just the sound of its name. If I hadn't talked Sheila into giving this town a second chance so we could be proud of it, she would still be alive right now.

"Maybe someday God will forgive you. And maybe someday when you're all rotting in hell you'll forgive yourselves. But Sheila and I never will. God help you all."

I walked away from the silent crowd; I put my arm up across my eyes and leaned against a tree. The hurt I felt could never be duplicated or described by anyone. I wept and I prayed. I didn't hear the ambulance pull up and take my Sheila away. Away forever.

Now here I stand and all I have is memories. Some of them good, some bad. I know that I can no longer stay here. It would be just like a ghost town for me now without Sheila. I guess it's just how fate plays her cards and toys with our emotions that we find ourselves facing uncertain tomorrows. I wonder if man were given the wisdom and the knowledge to know what lies ahead would he act for the better? I doubt it.

108

There's nothing left here for me except maybe a story. Maybe someday I'll write of Sheila's joys and loves. Her pain and sadness. Her tenderness and her shame. Maybe no one will believe her story if I told it like it happened. But if someone did and they could live a new and happy ending to it, then maybe her death wouldn't have been in vain. Just maybe someone can salvage the love that was wasted. Maybe they can avoid some of the heartache and pain. Maybe, only maybe.

*   *   *

A lone tear rolled down his cheek as he picked up his grip and coat. Glancing over to the vacant lot one last time, he managed a smile. He looked up at the sky and noticed the dense clouds finally were breaking up and giving way to the warmth of a filtering sun. He continued his walk down Bloomgarden Avenue.

A bus stopped at the corner and opened its doors. He took one last look at Cedar Dale. Then he got on. He was leaving Cedar Dale but he was leaving his heart there. For it belonged to **a girl named Sheila.**